JERRY MAHONEY

My Rotten Stepbrother Ruined BEAUTY AND THE BEAST

STONE ARCH BOOKS
a capstone imprint

My Rotten Stepbrother Ruined Fairy Tales is published by
Stone Arch Books, A Capstone Imprint
1710 Roe Crest Drive
North Mankato, Minnesota 56003
www.mycapstone.com

Text © 2018 Jerry Mahoney
Illustrations © 2018 Stone Arch Books

Library of Congress Cataloging-in-Publication Data
Names: Mahoney, Jerry, 1971- author. Title: My rotten stepbrother ruined Beauty and the beast / by Jerry Mahoney. Description: North Mankato, Minnesota : Stone Arch Books, a Capstone imprint, [2017] | Series: My rotten stepbrother ruined fairy tales | Summary: While eleven-year-old Maddie McMatthew's stepbrother Holden has been a little more tolerable since their first adventure, at the Halloween party he breaks another fairy tale by saying Beauty would never have fallen for the ugly Beast—and once again the two children find themselves sucked into another story and faced with having to set things right if they want to get home.
Identifiers: LCCN 2016059072| ISBN 9781496544650 (library binding) | ISBN 9781496544698 (pbk.) | ISBN 9781496544810 (ebook (pdf))
Subjects: LCSH: Beauty and the beast (Tale)-Juvenile fiction. | Fairy tales. | Magic--Juvenile fiction. | Stepbrothers--Juvenile fiction. | Brothers and sisters--Juvenile fiction. | CYAC: Characters in literature-Fiction. | Fairy tales-Fiction. | Magic-Fiction. | Stepbrothers-Fiction. | Brothers and sisters-Fiction.
Classification: LCC PZ7.1.M3467 Mu 2017 | DDC 813.6 [Fic] --dc23
LC record available at https://lccn.loc.gov/2016059072

Illustrations: Aleksei Bitskoff

Designer: Ashlee Suker

Printed in the United States of America.
010718R

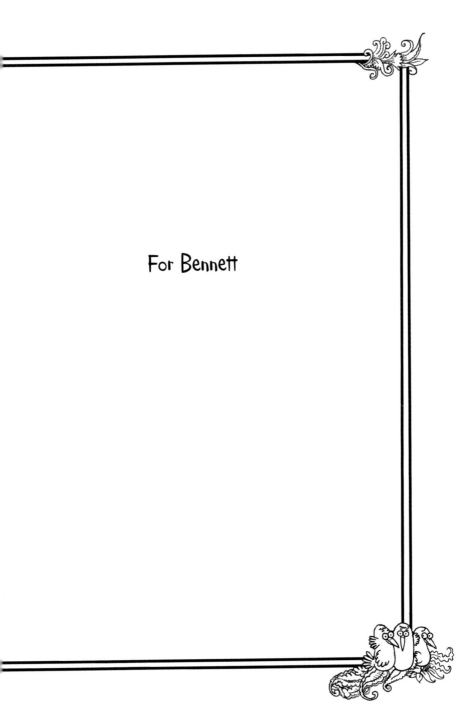

For Bennett

Chapter 1

Ever since he helped her save Cinderella, Maddie's stepbrother, Holden, had been surprisingly less horrible to her than usual. Giving a fairy tale back its Happily Ever After turned out to be a big bonding experience for the two stepsiblings, who until then, had never gotten along.

No one was happier to see them tolerating each other than their parents. Maddie's dad, Greg, and her stepmom, Carol, had only been married a few months, and they didn't like it when their kids' fighting intruded on their newlywed bliss. Even Maddie had to admit their middle-aged puppy love was a little overboard. The two of them kissed like teenagers every chance they got, constantly giggling about things only they found funny.

As nice as it was to see her dad happy, Maddie was looking forward to the day when he and Carol would settle in and start acting more like other people's parents. There were times Maddie didn't even recognize her father anymore.

He ate sushi now. (It was Carol's favorite food.) He took ballroom dancing lessons. (Also her idea.) Strangest of all, he was planning to dress up for Halloween for the first time in Maddie's life. He had always been one of those people who just left a bowl of candy on the front stoop with a sign that said, "Take one." If he could have wiped October thirty-first off the calendar, he probably would have. Then, along came Carol. She suggested they dress up as some eighties band called the Eurythmics, and suddenly, her dad couldn't wait for Halloween.

Carol had made herself a suit and tie and this bright orange crew cut wig to wear. Her dad had a shaggy fake beard and a wig that looked like it was made out of ratty brown poodle fur. The two of them were constantly sharing silly looks and singing about sweet dreams being made of "these," whatever that meant. Eighties bands were so weird.

Maddie loved Halloween because it was an annual opportunity for her to dress up as a fairy tale princess. This year, she wanted to go as Belle from *Beauty and the Beast*. Carol loved the idea and offered to help Maddie make the costume. Together, they went fabric shopping, and they picked out a beautiful tan taffeta, with some gorgeous yet comfortable shoes to go with it. Maddie really enjoyed spending time with Carol, who was so positive and upbeat it was hard to imagine how she ever raised such an obnoxious creep as Holden.

Maddie's stepbrother had no interest in Halloween, but Carol insisted. "You have to wear a costume to the school party," she said. "What are you going to go as?"

"I'll go as someone who doesn't care," Holden replied, rolling his eyes and walking away.

Carol leaned into Maddie and whispered, "If you're Beauty, maybe he should be the Beast."

She didn't realize Holden overheard her. "That's a great idea!" he called out.

"Oh, I'm just teasing, honey," Carol said.

"No, really," Holden replied. "I'd love to go as the Beast."

Maddie was stunned. Holden, the guy who couldn't stand fairy tales, was willing to dress as a fairy tale character? And to match her costume, no less? Maybe Holden really had changed from their time in Cinderella's story.

Carol squealed with delight. "Well, then let's get to work on your costume!"

"That's okay," Holden said. "I'd like to make it myself."

Maddie should have realized at that moment that he was up to something.

On Halloween night, Maddie spent almost an hour getting ready. She wanted to look as much like Belle as possible, so she used her curling iron to shape her hair into gorgeous flowing waves. She danced in front of the mirror wearing the dress she and Carol had made. She felt just like Belle . . . almost. There was only one thing missing: makeup. Her father had a rule that she wasn't allowed to wear it until she was fifteen, even for Halloween. She was convinced that, without it, she still looked like a little girl.

Trying to make the best of it, Maddie made a grand entrance into the living room. She descended the stairs gracefully, while her dad and Carol were watching a cooking show on TV. (Another thing he never used to do.)

Carol covered her mouth and gasped when she saw her. All she could say was, "Wow!"

Maddie's dad got choked up. "I can't believe that's my little girl!" he gushed.

Maddie had to admit she felt fantastic. She rushed up to Carol and gave her a hug. "Thanks so much for your help!"

"Oh, honey!" Carol said. "You really are a beauty."

"You know what would make me look even more like Belle?" Maddie said. "If I could put on some lipstick, maybe a little blush." She smiled at her dad, pleading with her eyes.

"No way," he shot back. "You're only eleven. You're too young for makeup."

To Maddie, her fifteenth birthday seemed like a hundred years away. Sometimes she looked in the mirror and imagined what her face would look like made up, if it would make her feel prettier or more grown up.

Once, she downloaded an app that added makeup to her selfies. She tried to use it to show her dad how natural she would look with makeup, how it wasn't such a big deal. But he refused to even look at the pictures. "Not until you're fifteen!" he insisted.

Carol knew it was a sore point, so she tried to change the subject. "I wouldn't be surprised if you win an award at the school party," she said. "Maybe you and Holden will even get Best Duo!"

"Well, that depends on how hard Holden actually worked on his costume." Maddie had no idea what to expect from him. He had been so secretive about what he'd been making, none of them had even caught a glimpse of it. In all likelihood, he wasn't even making a costume at all. He probably just picked up a rubber zombie mask at Spooky City and wrote "Hello, My Name Is Beast" on a nametag. That would be so like him, to do a half-hearted job after she had put so much effort into looking like Belle.

"I just hope he remembered to do it at all," Maddie said.

"How could I forget?" said an eerie voice behind her.

Maddie jolted from shock. "Holden, don't sneak up on — AAAH!" Maddie jolted even more when she turned around and got a look at Holden's costume. She couldn't remember the last time she had let out a legitimate scream of terror like that, but Holden's costume certainly warranted it.

He was far beastlier than anyone expected. He had fiery red eyes and razor-sharp fangs that dripped fake blood. Half his head was covered with fur. The other half was a bloody, exposed skull. All up and down his body were gashes and scars, as if he had just come from a vicious fight with another creature even more fearsome than he was.

It was all so realistic that Maddie had to catch her breath before she could yell at him. "Holden, you almost gave me a heart attack in that outfit!"

"Cool!" Holden said. "So you like it?"

"You don't look like the Beast!" Maddie huffed. "You look terrifying!"

"But that's the point. He's a beast. Beasts are scary. Except to Belle, of course. You're supposed to think this is hot stuff." He struck a pose, as if he were a model.

Maddie sighed. "I thought you wanted to dress up with me to be nice. I should've known better."

"Holden, take that costume off," Carol agreed.

"Well, so much for beauty only being skin deep," Holden shrugged. "Hey, tell me again why Belle fell in love with the Beast."

Maddie rolled her eyes. "Because he was a gentleman, unlike you. A decent person."

"Right," Holden said. "Like most kidnappers."

"He wasn't a kidnapper!"

"He held her in his castle against her will. And you believe her love for him was legit? I guess you've never heard of Stockholm Syndrome. That's where prisoners fall in love with their kidnappers. It's totally messed up, but that's probably the only reason why Belle fell for the Beast. I mean, what other choice did she have? She wasn't allowed to see any other men."

"It was true love!" Maddie insisted.

"Right, and he loved her for her heart, not because she was the prettiest woman in the kingdom. I guess the curse taught him nothing. He still fell for someone based on her looks."

Maddie's dad stepped in between them. "Guys, that's enough. Please don't argue about another fairy tale."

Maddie was furious. "He did this on purpose, Dad. He had no intention of making a costume. He just wanted to make a point!"

"I don't want to argue," Holden said, putting his mask back on. "I just want to go to the party."

"Not like that," Carol said, grabbing him by the shoulder. "If Maddie's not allowed to go outside wearing makeup, then you're not allowed to go out . . ." — she took another disgusted look at his costume — ". . . with half your skull exposed."

Maddie raised her hand to her face to cover up the fact that she was smiling. She loved to see Holden get in trouble.

"What am I supposed to wear then? I don't have another costume."

"Wear the suit you wore to our wedding," Dad said. "You looked very nice in that. You can say you're a lawyer."

Holden groaned. "Lame!"

"Don't feel bad, Holden," Maddie said. "No matter what you wear, you'll still be a beast on the inside."

Maddie's dad shot her an angry look. "If I hear one more comment like that, neither of you is going to the party!"

Maddie kept her mouth shut, but she couldn't help smirking at Holden as he went upstairs to get changed. It served him right for trying to ruin her Halloween and one of her favorite fairy tales.

Stockholm Syndrome? It made sense he would know so much about that, because the only way he'd ever get anyone to marry him is to kidnap them. Her rotten stepbrother didn't have a single romantic bone in his body. She didn't care what he said. She believed in true love, that Belle and the Beast were made for each other, and that they could look beyond their outward appearances and see that they were meant to be together.

Just like she and Holden were meant to be as far apart as possible.

Chapter 2

"I'm not sure that's how a necktie is supposed to look," Maddie said when Holden came downstairs for the Halloween dance.

She was trying to be polite, because in reality, his tie was an absolute disaster. The knot was the size of a fist, and the tie itself was crooked and only came halfway down his chest. Worst of all, he hadn't tucked it under his collar, so it was visible all the way around his neck.

"What?" Holden said defensively. "Looks okay to me."

"Here, let me help," Maddie's dad said. While he retied it, Holden reached down and grabbed his tablet, tucking it inside his suit coat.

"I doubt you'll need a tablet at the dance," Carol said.

"It's part of the costume," Holden insisted. "Lawyers don't go anywhere without their tablets these days."

Carol rolled her eyes. "Fine, just promise you won't spend the whole dance sitting in a corner playing video games."

Holden held his hand on his briefcase, as if taking an oath in court. "You have my solemn vow," he assured her. What a ham.

As soon as Holden and Maddie got dropped off, they walked in opposite directions. Neither of them wanted to be seen arriving at the dance with the other.

It wasn't long before a zombie and a ninja staggered up to Holden. "Nice costume," the ninja sneered. It was Holden's buddy Jamal, and even though nothing was showing through his face mask but his eyes, Holden could sense the sarcasm in his expression.

"I'll show you a nice costume," Holden replied, pulling out the tablet. He showed the photo of him in his Beast outfit.

"Whoa!" Jamal said. "That's sick!"

"Why didn't you wear that?" the zombie asked.

"My annoying stepsister," Holden jeered. "She had to go and make a big deal about it."

As Maddie scanned the dimly lit gym, she quickly noticed she wasn't the only Belle. Lauren Singer was also dressed as the famous princess, as was Abby Chou. Two other people in the same costume? Maddie was crestfallen. She thought about bolting and hiding under the bleachers by the football field until her dad came to pick her up in three hours. It was too late, though. She'd been spotted.

"Maddie? OMG!" The Cat in the Hat came running across the dance floor toward her. It took Maddie a moment to realize it was her friend Tasha.

"I can't believe there are other Belles," Maddie said.

"So what? Your costume blows theirs away."

"Thanks. My stepmom helped me make it. So I don't need to leave and go hide under the bleachers?"

Tasha laughed. "If the real Belle were here and she saw you, she'd go hide under the bleachers so she wouldn't get compared to you."

Tasha was a great friend who always knew how to cheer Maddie up. What really surprised Maddie is that everyone else gave her compliments, too. One kid said she was "fierce." Another told her she "rocked the Belle look."

A chaperone told her how grown-up she looked.

It seemed like everyone wanted to tell Maddie how pretty she looked. Girls, teachers. She even heard a few boys whisper about it when she walked by. "Check out Maddie McMatthews," one guy said to his friend.

"Whoa!" the friend replied.

In middle school, that's pretty much a rave review.

Holden had a great time, too, because he never stopped showing people the picture of himself in the Beast outfit. His friends thought it was awesome, but not everyone agreed. Two girls found the costume so disgusting they ran away screaming. Principal Montez agreed there was no way she would have let him into the party in such a repulsive outfit.

"Then you're no better than the Beast himself," Holden told her. "You judged my costume based on how it looked, rather than who was underneath it."

Principal Montez was not amused. "Well, anyone who came to this party wearing that costume would've been asked to take it off, and I would've given the person underneath it a week of detention."

That's when Holden remembered an important rule of middle school: never argue with the principal.

At the end of the night, the president of the student body got up to hand out awards for the best costumes. When they got to the prize for Prettiest Costume, she said it was no contest. "Maddie McMatthews!" she announced. Maddie felt bad for the other two girls who dressed as Belle, but they were both gracious in defeat.

Holden got an award, too — for Lamest Costume. He even beat out three people who weren't wearing costumes at all. "I'll show you what *should've* won best costume," he said as he accepted his booby prize. He pulled out his tablet, and he was about to show everyone the picture of his Beast costume when he saw Principal Montez shaking her head at the back of the gym.

"Um, check my Instagram," he said, quickly hiding the tablet from sight.

Maddie felt a little bad for her stepbrother, but only until he started gloating on the car ride home. "Did you hear those two girls screaming when I showed them the picture?" he asked. "I bet if I'd worn the costume, I could've gotten them to puke all over the dance floor!"

When they got home, Maddie's dad went immediately up to bed. He was exhausted from handing out candy to all the trick-or-treaters and constantly having to explain to them who the Eurythmics were. "I knew there was a reason I didn't like Halloween," he griped.

Holden couldn't wait to get out of his suit. "When I grow up," he said, "I'm getting a job where I don't have to wear one of these three-piece straightjackets every day."

As Holden took off his suit jacket, he placed his tablet down on the staircase, and the brightly lit screen illuminated the dark hallway. "That's weird," he said, picking it back up. "It should've done an auto shutdown by now." As Holden checked out the screen, he got a grave look on his face. "Um, Maddie, you should probably see this."

Maddie took a look at the screen. "I'm not looking at your Beast costume again. Let it go, Holden!"

"That's not it. I think I broke it."

"You broke your tablet?"

"No. The story. Look."

He pointed to an illustration on the screen, of Belle and Beast at their wedding.

Maddie shrugged. "They're getting married. Looks like a happily ever after to me."

"But isn't the Beast supposed to change back into a human at the end? Why is he still beastly?"

"You're right. That's weird." Maddie swiped through the pages on the tablet and saw new pictures she hadn't seen before. In one, Belle was crying. In another, she was dating a different man. "Holden! What have you done?" she said.

"Let me see." Holden took the tablet from her and flipped back to the first page of the story. "Well, at least it still starts off the same. 'Once upon a —'"

"Holden, no!" Maddie said, trying to stop him before he finished the phrase.

"— time," Holden said. Then, he looked at Maddie, confused. "What?"

A huge flash of light surged from the tablet, and Maddie and Holden each began to feel an odd tingling sensation. "Oh, no!" Holden shouted, realizing what was going on.

The two stepsiblings' bodies began to shrink and float across the room. Soon, they disappeared into the glowing screen. On the tablet, the cover illustration changed. Instead of Belle and the Beast dancing, it was a picture of Maddie and Holden amid a white background, both of them suddenly anticipating an adventure.

Chapter 3

Whiteness.

That was all that existed in every direction Maddie could see.

Whiteness and Holden, smirking like a nitwit.

The whiteness might have confused Maddie if she hadn't been in a place just like this once before, when she and Holden were transported into *Cinderella*. This time, she knew where she was: on a blank page, about to be filled with images and ideas. At any moment, words would start flying past them and filling out the story.

Maddie only hoped the first word would be *strangle*, so she could do to her stepbrother what she felt he deserved.

Instead, she saw two words, each beginning with a capital *B*. As they came closer, she was able to make out what they said. One was *Beauty*. The other, *Beast*.

Now she had a new hope: that the word *Beast* was headed right for Holden and would soon transform him into a revolting monster. He wouldn't think it was so funny if his disfigurement was more than just a costume, if it was a body he had to live in all the time. Then maybe he would understand what this fairy tale was all about.

Unfortunately, *Beast* flew right past Holden and into the background. Maddie sighed, though her disappointment didn't last long, as she saw that the other word, *Beauty*, was headed right for her.

Soon, she was transformed into a gorgeous young woman, every inch of her body sheer perfection. She wore an elegant white gown, her hair flowing delicately down her back in swooping brown curls.

A thousand more words rushed toward her, each of them with a single meaning. *Gorgeous, alluring, dazzling, stunning, ravishing, bewitching.*

With each new adjective, she became impossibly even more beautiful. There was no doubt about it. She was Belle.

Maybe this trip into a fairy tale wouldn't be so bad after all.

Other words began to fly past, filling in the scenery. *France, village, lawyer, castle.*

Wait a second. *Lawyer?* There was no lawyer in *Beauty and the Beast.*

The word settled over Holden's head and hung there as Holden transformed into a grown man in a sleek suit, a briefcase at his side. Soon, Holden faded from view, and Maddie was left wondering what role he could possibly play in this story.

Flowers, garden, altar, lavish. More words flew overhead, and from out of the whiteness grew an immaculate garden in the shadow of the most majestic castle Maddie had ever seen. Everything within view was oddly blurry, though, as if the world had yet to come into full focus.

A string quartet played a lush melody as scores of guests all turned at once and stared directly at Maddie. She was standing at the back of a long red carpet strewn with rose petals. She followed it up with her eyes and saw that it led to a glorious altar.

Suddenly Maddie realized why the world looked blurry. It wasn't because it had yet to come into focus. There was something blocking her view.

A veil.

Maddie took another look down at the long, white dress she was wearing.

It was a wedding dress.

In her hands, she held a colorful bouquet, and on her feet, she wore elegant bejeweled shoes.

This wasn't just any wedding. This was Belle's wedding. And everyone was waiting for her to walk down the aisle.

Chapter 4

Many young girls dream about their wedding day, and many of them picture theirs like a wedding from a fairy tale. Not many of them actually get to have a wedding in a fairy tale — at age eleven, no less.

Maddie marched gracefully down the aisle, relishing the magical moment. It was like getting a sneak preview of the happiest day of her life, and everything was perfect. Her dress was perfect. The scenery was perfect. The air was crisp and clear, and she could see for miles across the kingdom from high on the hill where the Beast's castle stood.

To her left, an artist painted the scene. Against the ice-blue sky, he was presently filling in the gazebo inside which the altar stood.

An old man led Maddie by the arm, smiling at her proudly as he escorted her to her groom. She knew this must be Belle's father, the man who told the villagers about how the Beast had been keeping her captive in his castle.

How sweet that he was there to see his daughter marry the man she had fallen in love with.

Maddie looked around to see if she could find Holden among the guests. She really wanted to rub his face in this. He was nowhere to be seen, though, which was odd.

He was a lawyer. That much she knew. But where would a lawyer fit into this story? Maybe he was going to witness the marriage certificate.

When Maddie reached the altar, she lifted her sparkling veil and looked into the adoring face of the man she was about to marry.

It was hideous.

Unlike in the story, the Beast hadn't changed back to a human. He was still a monster, with tusks, horns, cloven hooves, and a hunched back. His whole body was covered with dark, spotted fur.

"You look exquisite," the Beast said tenderly as he gazed into her eyes.

Despite his grizzly appearance, Maddie could see in his face how much he loved Belle, so she smiled back at him.

"Thank you. You, too," she replied, trying to sound as sincere as possible.

Is this what Holden changed about the story? she wondered. So the Beast remained ugly. Big deal. She was still going to marry him. The point, after all, was that Belle loved the Beast despite his grotesque appearance. That hadn't changed. All she had to do was say, "I do," and these two timeless characters would have their happily ever after. Then Maddie could go back home, along with Holden, wherever he was.

The Beast took Maddie's hand, bowed down, and placed a gentle, loving kiss on the back of it. It was so romantic, Maddie nearly fainted. This may not have been her life she was living, but she was determined to enjoy it while she was here.

The music stopped, and a hush fell over the room as the man at the altar started the ceremony.

"Dearly beloved . . . ," he began.

Unfortunately, that was as far as he got.

"Halt this wedding!" a man shouted. Maddie and the Beast gasped as soldiers surrounded the altar, swords drawn. "We've come for the Beast!"

Oh, darn, Maddie thought. It looked like this wasn't going to be so simple after all.

The men rushed in to subdue the Beast. Belle's father grabbed Maddie and took her aside, away from the siege. "Finally!" he whispered. "I thought they'd never arrive!"

"You're under arrest for kidnapping!" a soldier shouted as he led the Beast away.

"No, stop!" Maddie shouted. "You're ruining the story! I mean, the wedding!" She tried to run to the Beast, but Belle's father held her back.

"Stay with me!" he told her. "They'll get that horrible monster away from you!"

"He's not a monster!" Maddie replied. "You don't know what happened in the castle!"

"Yes, I do," Belle's father said. "He brainwashed you. And we're saving you, sweetheart."

Maddie saw that the painter had updated his work to depict the Beast being led away in disgrace. She watched in horror as soldiers lifted him into the back of a horse cart to take him to jail.

They clattered down the road to the village, and Maddie very clearly heard him say two things as he disappeared from sight.

The first was, "I love you, Belle!"

The second was, "Get me my lawyer!"

Maddie groaned. She knew exactly who that lawyer was going to be.

Chapter 5

Holden found himself sitting behind a desk in a weird office full of French dudes. He had seen the word *lawyer* floating above him a moment earlier, so he figured this was probably some kind of law firm and he was probably some kind of lawyer.

This was a little upsetting for him for two reasons: one, he didn't know anything about practicing law, and two, all the contracts laid out in front of him were in French. He had picked up a bit of French from that exchange student who came to their school last year, but mostly just *bonjour, au revoir,* and a few curse words.

If anyone in this dumb fairy tale expected him to actually speak the language, he was going to be in deep *poupe.*

A man poked his head into Holden's office. "Monsieur Rousseau!" he said. Rats, it was starting already. He needed to think fast.

"Um . . . croissant?" Holden said. "*Crêpes suzette?*"

He could only hope the man was asking him for his lunch order.

"What are you talking about?" the man replied.

"Oh, good. You speak English?"

"Of course," the man replied, confused. "We always talk in English here in this secluded French village."

"Whew!" Holden sighed. It made sense, he figured. Lots of fairy tales were set in places where they spoke other languages, but the characters always spoke English, at least in all the versions he ever read.

"Your client has asked for you," continued the man. "Monsieur de Maupassant."

"Mesher what? I thought we weren't doing the French thing," said Holden.

"Monsieur de Maupassant. Your client? The Beast."

"Oh, right! Him. Mesher duh . . . duh mow . . . duh moo?" Holden tried his best to pronounce the name, but he could tell from the look on the other man's face that he wasn't getting it. "Whatever. We'll call him Beast. Let's roll." Holden stood up to leave.

The man looked at him like he was crazy. "Why would we roll when we can walk?" he asked.

Even if they were all speaking English, Holden realized there was still going to be a language barrier to overcome.

Holden soon found himself in a small village jail. There was just one cell, and the man who was in it took up nearly half the space. He was facing the wall when Holden entered, but Holden could hear him snarling, and he knew right away who it was.

"Mesher What's-your-name?" Holden asked.

"I've been waiting for you," the prisoner said, and turned around. Holden got his first look at the Beast. He was massive, hairy, and incredibly hard to look at. Still, Holden was unimpressed.

"My costume was better," he bragged.

"What costume are you talking about, Monsieur Rousseau?" asked Beast.

"Never mind," Holden replied. "And you don't have to be so formal. Call me Holden, okay?"

"But your name is —"

"Just call me Holden," Holden interrupted. "I know we're in France, and this won't make a lot of sense, but I'm not so good at pronouncing French names. I just go by Holden."

"Okay, Holden," Beast said. "And you can call me Monsieur Patrice de Maupassant."

"How about Beast? I mean, let's not sugarcoat it, right? That's what everyone else calls you."

The Beast nodded humbly. "Very well. May we discuss my strategy for fighting the kidnapping charge?"

"Fight it?! You really think you can fight against a kidnapping charge?"

"I must!" the Beast said. "If I'm forced to live apart from Belle, I shall be too miserable to carry on!"

"But you did it. You kidnapped her."

"I love her!"

"It's still kidnapping!" Holden insisted. "You kept her in your house. She wasn't allowed to leave. Dude, that's jacked." Holden realized what good arguments he was making and determined he would probably be a very good lawyer.

"But she loves me, too!"

"Duh!" Holden said. "You're the only guy she ever saw. I guess if you keep someone in captivity long enough, even a beast starts to look like a dreamboat."

The Beast hung his head. "So what they're saying is true. I brainwashed her?"

"I call 'em like I see 'em," Holden agreed.

"Then I must be imprisoned," Beast said, "so Belle will never lay eyes on me again. I would rather live the remainder of my days in agony and loneliness than hurt her one more time."

The Beast shielded his face, and Holden realized he was crying. Holden couldn't believe it, but he was starting to feel bad for the guy.

"Look, I know you didn't mean to hurt her," Holden said. "Girls get really sensitive sometimes, you know?"

The Beast was unable to speak, he was crying so hard now. Holden thought about how much his mom cried when his dad moved out. He couldn't bear to listen to it.

"You really love her, don't you?" Holden said.

The Beast nodded softly as he wept.

"Okay," Holden said. "Then let's fight these charges."

"But you said I was guilty," the Beast said.

"That's for the judge to decide. Why not? It'll be fun."

Now Holden was picturing himself arguing in court, just like lawyers on TV. He barely noticed the Beast's crying anymore. He thought about how cool it would feel to stand up in front of a judge and shout, "Objection!"

and "Order in the court!" and "Permission to treat this as a hostile witness!" Holden smiled. Going to court sounded pretty sweet.

Chapter
6

Belle's father pulled his horse-drawn carriage up a hillside to a trim little cottage, then came to a stop out front. Beside him, Maddie stared in awe at the lush French countryside, with deep green fields flecked by brilliant patches of sunflowers. Everything was as bright and wondrous as the most magnificent storybook illustration.

Maddie stepped down from the carriage and onto a winding stone walkway that led through an ivy-wrapped gate to a rounded red door. On the rooftop, a cozy chimney sent perfect rings of smoke wafting up to the clear blue skies overhead. Carol was always watching real estate shows on TV, but even the most magnificent mansions Maddie had seen on those programs paled in comparison to the charm of this house.

It was Maddie's dream home.

"Do we live here?" she asked, breathless.

Belle's father shook his head, deeply concerned.

"So you don't even remember our home?" he asked. "I'm glad I invited Jeanette to talk to you."

"Jeanette?" Maddie said. She didn't remember anyone in *Beauty and the Beast* named Jeanette.

As Belle's father opened the front door, Maddie saw a small woman in glasses sitting with her legs crossed, her lips pressed into a tight smile.

"Hello, Belle," the woman said. "Why don't you have a seat and tell me about your childhood?"

Jeanette waved her hand toward a fainting couch, and it became clear to Maddie why this woman was there.

"You hired a therapist?" Maddie asked Belle's father.

"The Beast brainwashed you!" Belle's father said. "You don't even remember where we live!"

"Ugh," Maddie groaned. "Why does Holden have to ruin everything?"

"See what I mean?" Belle's father said to Jeanette. "Holden? That's not even the Beast's name. She's not making any sense!"

Jeanette nodded and wrote something down on a small notepad she had in her lap.

"What are you writing?" Maddie asked. "Is that about

me?" She tried to peek, but Jeanette blocked the notepad with her hand.

"The notes are for me, not you," she replied.

"Fine," Maddie said, sitting on the couch across from Jeanette. "I'll prove to you that Belle is totally fine and sane and in love."

"You mean you?" Jeanette asked.

"Huh?"

"You said Belle is fine. You know you're Belle, right?"

Maddie sighed. "Right. I'm Belle." She saw Belle's father and Jeanette both looking at her with great concern. Then Jeanette scribbled on her notepad again. "I swear I'm not crazy!"

"All right, then tell me about being kidnapped."

"That's not the word I would use to describe it," Maddie said. "That's Holden's word." Again, she received concerned looks from Belle's father and Jeanette. Again, Jeanette wrote on her notepad. She decided it was best not to mention Holden again. "I mean, that's how some people see what happened to me, but it wasn't like that."

"Then tell me how it was," Jeanette said. "How did he treat you when you first arrived at his castle?"

"When I first arrived?" Maddie frowned. "Okay, when I first arrived, he was kind of . . . not very nice. He kept me locked up. He yelled a lot. He said I'd be there forever."

Jeanette nodded along as she listened. "And when did you start to love this creature?"

"When you say it like that, Belle does sound crazy. I mean, I sound crazy. I mean, he turned out to be really nice. He danced with me. He made romantic dinners."

"Can you think of any reason why he started treating you well?"

"No," Maddie said, but it was clear from her face that she could. "Well, okay, he did kind of need me to fall in love with him so it would break his spell."

"So he tricked you into loving him."

"No!" Maddie protested. "I don't think so."

Jeanette nodded gently, as if she was hearing exactly what she expected to. "Describe the feelings you had for this creature."

"You want me to describe how love feels?" Maddie couldn't help giggling.

"Can you?"

"Well, no. I mean, I'm only — I've read about love, but . . ."

Maddie blushed. She was only eleven years old. How could she ever describe what love was like?

"But you're sure that you loved him?" Jeanette asked.

"I guess I can't be totally one hundred percent sure."

Belle's father leapt up and clapped his hands in delight. "It's a breakthrough!" he exclaimed.

"Don't you think you owe it to yourself to find out if your feelings were real?" Jeanette asked. And then she added, "To Belle?"

Maddie gazed across the room and spotted her reflection in a mirror. It was her first time seeing Belle's face. It was the very vision of beauty. But she saw something else in her expression: uncertainty. "I guess I do," she admitted.

Chapter
7

Holden was amazed how many people showed up at court to watch the Beast's trial. There were businessmen and beggars. Schoolgirls and little old ladies. They were all different types, but every one of them looked nice and perfectly reasonable, like friendly storybook characters. They chatted quietly with each other as they waited for the judge and the defendant to take their places. *Convincing these good-hearted country folk to set the Beast free will be a piece of cake,* Holden thought.

An officer of the court stood up and called everyone to attention. "All rise for the judge, the honorable Hercule Moreau," he said.

Everyone stood respectfully as Judge Moreau entered. "No, please, sit! Sit!" he said, embarrassed by all the attention. He was an older man, with kind eyes and a warm expression. He seemed like somebody's grandpa. Holden could picture him playing airplane with a toddler or recording his grandkid's school play on a really old camcorder. What he couldn't picture him doing was sentencing someone for kidnapping. Not this sweet old man, no way.

"*Bonjour*, everyone," Judge Moreau said cheerfully, as the spectators all sat back down. "Thank you all for coming. It certainly is a lovely day for a trial." He looked through the papers on his desk. "Now let's see what the charge is today. Ooh, kidnapping! Yes, the pretty girl in the castle. I remember hearing about this case. What a tale!"

Holden smiled. This was almost going to be too easy.

"I guess we should bring in the defendant then," Judge Moreau said. "Hopefully, we can clear this mess up once and for all." A door in the back of the courtroom opened, and two guards led the Beast into the room, shackled and sad. Instantly, the calm mood of the room was upended. People stood up again, but this time, it wasn't out of respect.

"Boo!" they jeered. "He's a monster!" "Look at him!" "He's clearly guilty!"

The Beast hung his head. Holden was flabbergasted at how quickly the crowd changed when they saw him. These nice French village folk turned into raging nutjobs. He'd thought at least the schoolgirls would be on his side. They should be like Maddie, naïve and romantic, so ready to believe in true love.

Instead, they were some of the ones denouncing the Beast the loudest. "Freak!" they shouted. "Savage!"

"Objection!" Holden called out amid the chaos.

The judge stared at him, baffled. "What are you objecting to?"

"They're being jerks."

"Overruled," the judge responded. He mouthed the word *sorry* to Holden. Holden was tempted to stick his tongue out at him in return, but he figured that wouldn't go over well. "Now, let's talk to the kidnapper," Judge Moreau continued. "I mean, the defendant." Holden sighed. Even the judge seemed to be against him now. "Monsieur de Maupassant, how do you plead?"

"Totally not guilty," Holden said, answering for the Beast. Again, an uproar came from the spectators, and the judge had to bang his gavel to calm them down.

Holden scanned the faces of the spectators, and all of them were gazing at the Beast in disgust. It wasn't fair. They didn't even know what had happened. They were judging the Beast solely based on how he looked. Holden was more determined than ever to help him beat this charge.

The judge waited patiently for everyone to quiet down so he could speak again. "Well, I think everyone needs to calm down a bit before we hear all the nasty details of this case. How about we call it a day, everyone get some rest, and we'll start arguments tomorrow at . . . let's say noon-ish. Sound good?"

Holden was relieved. Now he'd have time to prepare his case. Maybe the judge was on his side after all.

"And if the defendant is found guilty," Judge Moreau continued, "he will be beheaded in the evening." He banged his gavel, stood up, and left the bench.

Man, Holden thought. *Fairy tale justice is harsh.*

Chapter 8

After talking with Jeanette all afternoon, Maddie was desperate to see the Beast. She wondered if she would feel a spark or see fireworks or do any of the things people supposedly did when they were in love. More importantly, would she be able to tell if his feelings for her were real? Or if he was merely tricking her to break his spell?

She walked down to the village so she could visit him in his jail cell. Though she was nervous about the outcome of Belle and the Beast's tale, she couldn't help but be enraptured by the world she found herself in. Adorable little houses dotted the hillsides. Chittering forest creatures scampered to and fro and seemed to smile at her as she walked by. She heard birds singing joyous songs from high in the treetops and fish splashing as they leapt in and out of a bubbling brook.

When Maddie reached the village, everyone was delighted to see Belle and immediately stopped what they were doing to say hello. A woman ran out of a pottery store with clay all over her hands so that she could wave. "Hello, Belle!" she called. "So good to see you!"

People came out of every shop Maddie walked past. A kind old man at the hat shop whipped off his beret and bowed to her. "Dear, sweet Belle!" he said, kissing the back of her hand.

"Well, hi!" Maddie replied.

In the town square, a man playing the lute for some dancing children paused in the middle of his song. "Look, everyone! Belle is here!" The children all ran up to Maddie and danced around her in a ring, giggling happily.

A glass blower was so blown away by the sight of Belle that he dropped the vase he was making and shattered it.

"Belle!" he cheered. "So nice to see you!"

Soon, Maddie reached a cozy little café, and a baker darted up to her with a plate of piping hot food.

"Belle!" he said. "Sit. I've made your favorite quiche!"

"Oh, that's so nice," Maddie said, "but I didn't bring any money with me."

"Pfft!" the baker tutted, pulling out a chair for her. "As if I'd ever make my favorite customer pay!"

Free food? Maddie couldn't imagine getting free food back in the real world. People obviously really liked Belle. Even though she was on her way to see the Beast, she didn't want to insult the baker, so she sat down and took a bite of his quiche. It was the most delicious thing she had ever tasted. "Mmm! I love it!" she said, taking another bite.

Before she even realized it, Maddie had eaten the whole quiche, and the baker was presenting her with a tray of pastries for dessert. "Take your pick!" he exclaimed.

"That's really nice," Maddie said. "But I should go."

"Well, you come back to Café LeGrande any time, dear," the baker replied. "It's always good to see you, Belle."

Maddie continued walking down the lane and waving back to everyone she saw. Other people came to give her free things, too. A florist gave her a fresh-cut rose. A sweet-shop owner gave her a chocolate in the shape of a heart. A jewelry maker even gave her a beautiful necklace.

"But I can't accept something like this for free!" Maddie told her.

"I want you to!" the jeweler replied. "If people see you wearing the necklace I've made, they will all want to wear my designs!"

Maddie had never received so much attention before. It was very exciting. Just as she saw the jailhouse come into view, another villager stopped her.

"Pardon me, Belle," he said. His voice was as smooth as butter, with the most romantic French accent.

Maddie turned to get a look at his face, and when she saw him, she was speechless. He reminded her of Jake Templeton, the sixth grader all the girls thought was so cute. He was boyish but just a bit scruffy, with sweet, deep blue eyes and chiseled, firm biceps. He had dimples and a slick swoop of jet-black hair that swept over his forehead. He could have modeled for the cover of a romance novel or been in a boy band.

He was *that* handsome.

"Wh— wh— wh—," she stammered.

"It's so nice to see you safe and sound," he said. "All those months you were gone, I was so worried."

"You worried . . . about me?" Maddie said.

"I don't know how it's possible, but you're even more beautiful than when you left." The charismatic man flashed his sparkling blue eyes at Maddie. "You probably don't even remember me."

"You? Well, you're . . . you're . . ." Maddie didn't know him, of course. Whoever he was, he was never mentioned in the story. She would have remembered someone so handsome and charming who had taken such an interest in Belle.

"It's okay," he said. "I'm Beau, and just before you were kidnapped, you agreed to go on a date with me. It's all right, though, if you don't remember. I know you went through quite an ordeal."

Maddie wanted to pinch herself. Did she just get asked on a date? The boys at her school always got so weird around girls. When somebody liked you, you only heard about it when they told one of their friends, who told one of your friends, who passed you a note saying, "I think so-and-so likes you." And you were never sure if it was true or not. This was nothing like that. Beau liked her, no doubt. How cool.

Maddie thought about what Jeanette had said. Maybe she should date other men, just to see if her feelings for the Beast were real. Could it really hurt to have dinner with Beau?

Then she stopped herself. What was she thinking? She was just being shallow and falling for his good looks. This went directly against what the story was about. There was a character in this story she was supposed to date, and he wasn't a sweet, suave hunk. He was gigantic and covered in fur.

"I have to go see the Beast," Maddie said, turning away from Beau.

"Then let me escort you," Beau said, taking Maddie by the arm.

"You would do that?" she replied.

"I would do anything for you, Belle," he answered, and he led her down the street toward the jailhouse. Maddie had to admit, this guy was kind of a catch.

Chapter 9

Maddie was greeted at the jailhouse door by a guard. *Greeted* is the wrong word, actually, since the guard's first words were, "Go away!"

The guard was tall, broad-shouldered, and — it took Maddie a moment to realize — female. She was almost the exact opposite of Belle, with hard features and a vicious scowl. Her hair was pulled into a tight, no-nonsense bun, and she stood so perfectly still that, until she spoke, Maddie mistook her for a very lifelike statue.

"But I'm Belle!" Maddie protested.

It still sounded strange to say those words. She almost didn't believe it herself.

"I know who you are," the guard barked at her. "He has requested no visitors . . . especially you!"

It broke Maddie's heart to think that the Beast didn't want to see Belle. They had really messed up this fairy tale if that was the case. Seeing no way to get past the hulking guard, Maddie sulked around the corner. As she was wondering what to do now, she heard a man approaching the jailhouse.

"Yo, Simone," the man said.

Maddie was pretty sure that *yo* was not a French word, so she stayed to listen to the rest of their conversation.

"You wouldn't believe what they tried to sell me at that café," the man continued. "Snails! I mean, gross, right?"

"*Escargot* are my favorite!" the guard said.

"Whatev!" the man replied. "You Frenchies are cray-cray."

Maddie was pretty sure by now that she knew who this man was. But just to be certain, she peeked around the corner. He was dressed in a suit, but his tie was crooked and messy. It stuck way out from underneath his collar. He clearly didn't know how to tie it.

"Holden!" Maddie shouted. She ran around the corner to face him. "It's me!"

Holden gaped at her, surprised. "Maddie? Whoa, you look good!"

Simone the guard was very confused by their interaction. "Maddie?" the guard said. "No, Monsieur Rousseau. This is Belle."

"You're Belle?!" Holden said to Maddie. "No fair! I'm just a stinking lawyer."

"Holden, I desperately need you to get me in to see the Beast!" Maddie pleaded.

"Impossible!" Simone said. "He distinctly said not to let you in!"

"Aw, Simone, c'mon," Holden said. "She really needs to see him. I'll dig some snails out of the garden for you."

Simone rolled her eyes and stepped aside for them. "I'll give you five minutes," she said. "Be quick!"

"Mercy!" Holden said as he stepped past her.

"What?" Simone replied.

"He means *merci*," Maddie explained, using the French word for *thank you*. She wondered how Holden had been able to survive this long in the fairy tale without her.

As they walked down the hallway toward the Beast's cell, Holden bragged proudly, "That was awesome how I got her to let you in. I'm really good at persuading people. I'm a kick-butt lawyer."

"So you think you'll be able to get him freed?"

"I don't know," Holden admitted. "People really can't stand that guy."

"What do you mean? Everyone here seems so nice."

"Not to the Beast, they're not," Holden replied. "You should've seen the way they treated him in court. I don't know how to tell you this, but if I can't save him, tomorrow night they're going to chop his furry head off."

Maddie gasped. "They're really going to send him to the guillotine?"

Holden nodded. "Yup. This time tomorrow they can use his head for a soccer ball."

"Then we'd better hurry," Maddie said.

Holden walked her up to a cell, where a large hairy figure cowered in the corner.

"Uh . . . Beast?" Holden said. "I think you know this chick."

The Beast looked up, shocked to see Belle. "Belle, no!" he said. "I didn't want you to see me like this!"

Holden rolled his eyes. "Dude, you're covered in fur, with horns and tusks and totally nasty teeth. Is this really so much worse than what she's used to seeing?"

"I had to visit you," Maddie said, ignoring Holden.

The Beast shook his head. "Belle, you look . . . different."

"She looks a lot different than I'm used to, that's for sure," Holden joked. Maddie elbowed him, annoyed.

The Beast reached out a paw and tenderly caressed Maddie's cheek. "I mean, you look so sad."

"I heard people were being mean to you," Maddie said.

The Beast lowered his head and spoke in a voice barely above a whisper. "It's nothing I don't deserve after I brainwashed you. How could someone as beautiful as you ever love someone as ugly as me?"

"That's the whole point!" Maddie explained. "Beauty is only skin deep. What we have goes much deeper. If we stay together, we can prove it to the world."

The Beast shook his head. "I'm not sure I believe it myself. Belle, I think you should date someone else. Someone who's not a monster."

"No!" Maddie begged. "Please!"

"Time's up!" bellowed Simone, as she thundered down the hall. "*Au revoir*, pretty lady!"

"Wait! Beast, we're meant to be together!"

Simone grabbed Maddie and began to drag her away from the cell. The Beast took one last look at her as she disappeared down the hallway. "Prove to yourself that there's no other man for you," he called after her. "Only then will I agree to see you again."

The Beast turned away, and Simone shoved Maddie outside into the street. As the door swung shut behind her, Maddie ran away from the jail, covering her face so no one would see her cry.

Chapter
10

When Holden caught up with Maddie, she was almost at the edge of the village, and she looked seriously bummed out.

"What's up?" he asked, jogging up beside her.

"The Beast. He's so mean!" Maddie said. "What if Belle really wasn't supposed to fall in love with him?"

Holden shrugged. "So do it."

"Do what?"

"Go on a date. Play the field. Check out the scene." He pulled out his tablet. "There has to be a dating app on here somewhere. We'll set you up with a profile, put down what you're looking for, uncheck the box marked 'beasts.'"

"Holden! Put that away before someone sees it!" She pushed the tablet back down inside his coat. "Besides, you know Dad says I can't date until I'm sixteen!"

Holden rolled his eyes. "You're not *you* here, and your dad's not your dad. You have to do what Belle would do, and if we ever want to get home, she'd better fall in love with someone quick."

As Maddie thought this over, a horse-drawn carriage pulled up beside them. "Whoa!" called the driver, stopping his horses. "*Bonjour*, Belle! Can I give you a ride home?"

"That's so sweet!" Maddie said. "See, Holden? I told you people were nice here."

"Hold on a second," Holden said. "You're offering her a ride? For free?"

The man smiled warmly. "The only payment I ask is the company of a beautiful woman." He winked at Maddie.

"Well, I'm sorry," Holden said. "But this woman doesn't take rides from strangers."

"Very well then," the man said, tipping his hat. "It's a lovely day for a walk anyway. Let me know if you need anything, Belle." He yanked on the reins and started his horses up again.

As the carriage pulled away, Holden had a realization. "Hold on. That's why everyone's so nice to you," he said. "It's because you're pretty." Maddie giggled.

"What's so funny?" Holden asked. He really didn't understand his stepsister sometimes.

Maddie blushed. "You said I was pretty."

Holden groaned. "I'm talking about Belle. Belle is pretty. And that's why I need her to testify at the Beast's trial. They'll listen to her, because they like her."

"But the Beast said he didn't want to see me again unless . . ." Maddie sighed.

". . . you go on a date! So do it," Holden said. "C'mon. I won't tell your dad."

"Well, there is one guy who asked me out. He seemed nice."

"Perfect," Holden said. "Set it up." Holden waved goodbye and started to walk back into the village.

"What are you going to do?"

"I'm going to figure out how to get the Beast a fair trial." Holden only walked a few feet before he heard a loud growling sound. He looked down and realized it was the sound of his stomach. "But first," he said, "I'm going to get something to eat."

Holden was very disappointed with the restaurant options available in this fairy tale. He couldn't find a single place that served hamburgers or chicken fingers or foot-long subs. When he asked for a burrito, people looked at him like he was speaking a foreign language. He finally found a café where the patrons were eating croissants, so he figured he would order something there. Maybe a croissant with egg and bacon in the middle, something like what they served in fast food restaurants back home.

Holden got in line to order and decided he'd ask for some French toast sticks on the side. He wondered if he should just call them "toast sticks," since he was in France, after all. He had plenty of time to figure out what he wanted to say, because the guy in front of him in line was taking forever to order.

"Um, is this a shoe store?" the man said. He was young and well-dressed, but for some reason, he was incredibly confused.

"No, Monsieur Voltaire," the waiter behind the counter replied. "It is Café LeGrande."

"That's good," the man said, "because I forgot to wear my shoes."

Holden looked down and saw that the man was barefoot. Huh?

"Shall I make your usual lunch?" the waiter asked him.

"Lunch?" the man replied. "But it's after midnight."

Holden double-checked behind him. The sun was shining brightly. It was still clearly afternoon.

What was up with this guy?

"Have a seat, Monsieur," the waiter said, kindly. "I will take care of you."

The man turned around and wandered through the café aimlessly.

"Geez, what a wacko, huh?" Holden said to the waiter, then added, "Can I get a croissan'wich with some toast sticks?"

"Oh, no!" the waiter said. "Has it happened to you, too?"

"Has what happened?" Holden asked.

The waiter shook his head sadly as he gazed toward the confused man. "The fairy made you simple-minded?"

"Fairy? No . . . hey! I'm not simple-minded! Whatever that's supposed to mean."

"My apologies, sir. Monsieur Voltaire has been through quite an ordeal. He used to be the smartest man in town, but he was not very humble. He would mock people who weren't as intelligent as he was. He was so cruel. Then a magical fairy decided to teach him a lesson, and she made him less intelligent. Now, he can only regain his smarts if he gets a brilliant woman to fall in love with him."

"A fairy did that?" Holden asked.

"Yes, you've probably never heard anything like that before."

"Actually, I've heard something a lot like it," Holden said. "Just make me something other than snails, please."

He left the counter and followed the wandering man to a table on the sidewalk. "Mind if I take this seat?" he asked him.

"But where will you take it?" Monsieur Voltaire replied, scratching his head.

"No, I mean . . . I want to sit here." Holden sighed and decided to just sit down. "Listen, I heard what happened to you, and you got a raw deal, dude."

"I did?" said the man. "I thought everything they served here was cooked."

"No, not that kind of raw," Holden explained. "See, that fairy who put the spell on you, she messed with a guy I know, too. I was just wondering, do you remember her name?"

"I do!" the man said happily.

"Okay," Holden said, trying to be patient. "Can you tell it to me?"

"Tell you what?"

"The fairy's name."

The man hung his head, sadly. "I forgot."

Holden worried that getting any information out of this man could take all day. It probably wasn't worth trying.

Then, he heard a voice behind him. "Excuse me, were you just talking about Resplenda?"

"Resplenda?" Holden said, turning around.

"Yes, she's the fairy who did this to me." Holden looked at the man, who was the flabbiest, most out-of-shape person he had ever seen. There were huge bags of skin sagging from all over his body.

"Let me guess," Holden said. "You used to be really muscular, right? And kind of a jerk about it?"

The man nodded.

"Wow, this fairy really likes to teach people lessons, doesn't she? Okay, tell me where I can find this chick."

The man lowered his head, as if he feared to even speak of the fairy world. Then, he whispered his instructions. "The only known path to the fairy world is to head into the Dark Forest one hundred paces, until you reach a spot where nothing grows and the river runs backwards. Step into its current and make an impossible wish. Only then will the door to the fairy world open."

"Okay, back up. How do I find the Dark Forest?"

"Only the fairies know for sure, but they say the key is knowing where to look."

The man walked away, as the waiter arrived with Monsieur Voltaire's lunch. "I won't eat this!" Monsieur Voltaire said. "You haven't cooked it!"

Holden groaned and got up from the table. "Ugh, I hate fairy tales," he muttered.

Chapter 11

Everything Maddie knew about dating came from watching her dad get ready to go out with Carol. At first, he used to tell her he was going out "with a friend." But she noticed him doing things he didn't normally do when he went out with friends, like shower in the afternoon, put gel in his hair, and use aftershave lotion.

Maddie's grandma would come over to babysit, and she would say things to Maddie's dad like, "Hold the door for her," and, "Tell her she looks pretty." Her dad would roll his eyes and reply, "I know, Mom!" Even though she was only eight at the time, Maddie figured out pretty quickly that whoever her dad was seeing was more than just a friend.

Maddie tried not to be nervous getting ready for her own date, but it was all very overwhelming. It was the first date she would ever go on, even if it was really Belle's and not hers. Plus, Belle had so many gorgeous dresses to choose from, Maddie took half an hour just trying them all on and picking the one she liked best. Then she took another half hour picking out a pair of shoes. She was relieved she had the necklace from the jeweler because it saved her from another major decision.

Just as she finished getting ready, Maddie heard a carriage pull up outside the house. She peeked through the window and saw Belle's father greeting Beau by the gate. Beau looked very handsome and had a bouquet of flowers for her. She was so excited, she squealed with delight. Apparently, she was a little too loud, because Belle's father and Beau both looked over and saw her watching them from the window.

She quickly ducked away, and she could hear the men chuckling outside. So embarrassing!

She wondered where Beau would take her. What would they talk about? Should she tell him how much she loved gymnastics, and how her team made the regional finals last year? No, wait. She couldn't tell him that. She was Belle. She would have to talk about Belle's interests. Maybe she could recount all the things that happened to her in the Beast's castle. That was something Maddie knew a lot about, having read the story so many times.

There was a knock on the bedroom door, and Belle's father poked his head in. "Don't worry," he said. "I told him you needed some time to get ready."

"Nope," Maddie said. "I'm ready right now! Let's go!" She started to walk out of her bedroom, but Belle's father blocked the doorway.

"You can't be serious," he said. "You don't look ready to go out!"

Maddie checked herself in the mirror. She wasn't sure what he meant. The dress, her hair. Everything seemed perfectly in order. "I thought I looked good," she said.

"Sweetheart," Belle's father replied, "you always look good. But when you go on a date, you really need to knock a man's socks off! Let your hair down, put some makeup on."

"Makeup! No, I'm not allowed to wear makeup!" Maddie said, before she caught herself. She wasn't allowed to wear makeup, but surely Belle was.

Her father gasped. "What kind of beast wouldn't let you wear makeup?"

I call him Dad, Maddie thought to herself. She always hated her dad's "no makeup until you're fifteen" policy. So many of her friends were already putting on blush and lipstick for school every day, and Lisa LaDonovitz was already wearing mascara!

"You're right," Maddie said, finally. "I should wear makeup! But I'd better hurry, so I won't keep Beau waiting."

"He'll wait as long as he needs to," Belle's father assured her. "Maybe I can help you a bit."

He led Maddie over to Belle's vanity, where she excitedly checked out all of Belle's makeup. She couldn't wait to try it, but she wasn't sure exactly what to do with all of it. No one had ever taught her how to put on makeup. She picked up a powder puff and pressed it against her face, sending a cloud of powder all around her head. Overwhelmed, Maddie coughed on all the dust.

Belle's father shook his head. "It really has been a while, hasn't it? Well, don't worry, because I remember exactly how you used to get ready for dates. Sit down, sweetheart. I'll take care of everything!"

"Really?" Maddie said.

She couldn't believe how much cooler Belle's dad was than her own. She felt so liberated, so rebellious. She was going to wear makeup, and her dad couldn't stop her. This could be fun.

"Am I beautiful yet?" Maddie asked, annoyed. Putting on makeup got old fast, and it never seemed to end. She had been sitting at that vanity for over an hour now, while Belle's father delicately applied makeup to her face. He was acting as if he were an artist painting a canvas, though Maddie was pretty sure Michelangelo painted the entire Sistine Chapel faster than this.

Is this what women did when they got ready for dates? Did it really take this long? Was it really this boring? Maddie couldn't imagine it mattered that much to boys. She was certainly never going to do this herself when she started dating.

She also felt awful about keeping Beau waiting all this time, no matter how much her father assured her he would be happy once he saw how amazing Belle looked.

"And . . . done!" Belle's father said, with a final stroke of the mascara brush. "Your makeup is ready!"

"Thank goodness!" Maddie said. She started to stand up, but Belle's father put his hand on her shoulder, pushing her back down into the chair.

"Now, let's start on your hair!"

"My hair?!"

"Well, you can't just leave it like this!"

Groaning, Maddie sat back down. She was Belle, after all, so she had to do things the way Belle did. She only wished she had a magazine to read during all this never-ending primping.

Chapter 12

Holden wandered for hours searching for the Dark Forest, but everything in Belle's world was ridiculously bright and colorful. There were no clouds, there was no dirt, nothing rotten or gloomy in sight. Even as the sun set, the forests didn't seem to get any darker. He thought back to what the man at the café told him. "The key is knowing where to look."

What was that supposed to mean? How was he supposed to know where to look without a map or anything? Geez.

Worn out, Holden sat down on a rock to rest. He was hot and sweaty, so he took off his suit jacket. He opened his briefcase, hoping to cram it in there so he wouldn't have to carry it, but that's when he saw something else: his tablet.

Cool! He turned it on and flipped through the icons, wondering what to do first. Should he play *Astro Turbo Rush* or *Fudgie the Fox 4*? Maybe he could watch the new episode of *Zombie Bounty Hunter* — that is, if the fairy tale world had Wi-Fi. Either way, this was awesome. He wondered if he could wait this whole thing out in the woods. Maddie would probably fix the story on her own eventually, and in the meantime, he could level up his orc in *Clashes of War.*

Then he remembered how he had used his tablet when they were stuck in *Cinderella.* He looked at the e-book and saw illustrations from the story as it happened. Maybe that would work this time around, too. He swiped at the screen and looked at drawings from *Beauty and the Beast* as he and Maddie were rewriting it. There he was as a lawyer, shouting, "Objection!" in court. It looked even cooler than he imagined it would. Next, he saw Maddie, as Belle, going on a date — and wearing makeup! Ooh, her dad was going to be so mad!

Then, on the next page, he saw exactly what he was looking for: a map of the very woods he was stuck in, with the Dark Forest clearly marked. Sweet! Now he knew where to look.

He was so excited, he only stopped to play one game of *Fudgie the Fox 4* before heading off for the Dark Forest.

When Holden reached the location on the map, he knew right away he was at the Dark Forest. It was the first place he'd seen in this world that wasn't sunny and bright. Instead, there were massive willow trees casting shade over everything around. Their trunks curled in creepy shapes, like the faces of monsters laughing at him. Everything had a burned-out feel to it, as if the ground were made of ash.

"Ninety-eight . . . ninety-nine . . . one hundred." Holden counted his steps, and sure enough, when he had gone one hundred paces, he reached a clearing where no plants grew. The ground was desolate and bare, and in front of him stood a winding river. It ran in one direction as far as he could see, except for the spot directly at his feet. There, the water somehow flowed in the exact opposite direction. It defied all logic and laws of physics. It was . . . well, like something out of a fairy tale, which is how Holden knew he was in the right place.

He kicked off his shoes and pulled off his socks, then rolled up his pant legs and stepped into the water. He thought back to what the man said he had to do next. Make an impossible wish. Hmm . . . What could he wish for that would never actually happen?

"I wish Maddie would shut up for five seconds sometime," he said, laughing at his own joke.

Nothing happened.

"Just kidding," he said. "Let's see . . ." He thought harder. "I wish . . . I could get an A in math."

Again, nothing happened.

"Sweet!" he said. "I never thought that was possible."

It was encouraging, but if he wanted to reach the fairy world, he was going to have to try harder. He thought about what he would really wish for, at this very moment, if he could. Then, it came to him clearly.

"I wish I could get out of this cuckoo fairy tale without having to give it back its happily ever after."

Holden heard a great rumble, and then there was a flash of light. When his eyes readjusted, he saw a door on the opposite bank of the river. It was green and glowing, with fairy dust swirling around it.

"Yeah, I figured that wasn't going to happen." He sighed, and began to wade across the river toward the magic door to the fairy world.

Chapter 13

By the time Belle's father announced that Maddie was ready for her date, Maddie felt more like going to bed. Getting ready was so exhausting. She wasn't sure how she was going to summon the energy to go out with Beau.

Then Belle's father showed her a mirror. "Well, what do you think?" he asked.

Maddie took one look at her reflection and let out an enormous gasp. All that preparation had paid off.

She looked like she could appear on a TV show or in a music video!

"Wow," she said. It felt wonderful to be this beautiful. She couldn't wait for the date now.

When she came downstairs, Beau also gasped. "Am I dreaming, or is it really possible for one woman to possess so much beauty?"

Maddie was so flattered she couldn't help giggling. "I'm sorry," she said. "I know you've been waiting, like, forever."

"My dear," he said, "when I look at you now, I can no longer think of the past. All I see is the present, and a future that I hope will stretch on forever."

Ooh! He said such romantic things! Maddie tried not to giggle again. This was going to be a really fun night. Her first date, her first time wearing makeup. She decided at the end of the night, she would allow herself an even more exciting first experience: her first kiss!

Beau took Maddie to a majestic chateau in the mountains. Together, they watched the sun set from a private table on a balcony while a chef made them dinner. The view was incredible. The entire countryside seemed to be cast in a warm orange glow, as a silvery moon took the sun's place in the sky and day gave way to night.

"Wow," was all Maddie could seem to say. "I've never seen anything so beautiful."

Beau sat with his back to the sunset, facing Maddie. "I'm sure it's exquisite," he said, staring deeply at her, "yet I would not trade anything for the view I have just gazing into your eyes."

Maddie blushed. Once again, he had found an almost poetic way to compliment her appearance. This guy was so charming, whereas the Beast always stumbled over what to say. Maybe Beau was the right match for Belle after all.

Now that she had opened her mind to the possibility, Maddie figured she should get to know more about this guy. That's the only way she would know for sure. She thought about the kinds of things people said on dates and decided to start a conversation.

"So . . . what do you do for fun?" she asked him.

"Fun?" he said. "I'm not sure I ever truly knew what fun was until you stepped into my carriage tonight and embarked on this adventure with me."

Maddie smiled. Again with the smooth talk! "That's really nice," she said, "but have you ever gone bowling?"

"I am bowled over by the blue in your eyes," he said. "It is a blue so rich, so fine, I might forget there is anything else to do in this world but admire its perfection."

Okay, that was a bit much. It was nice to have someone tell her she was pretty, but didn't this guy have anything else to say? Maddie wondered if she would ever get a straight answer out of him. She decided to try something different. Maybe if she told him more about Belle, he would start asking the questions.

"I'll tell you what I like to do," she said. "I'm a big reader."

"I could write an entire book just about your cheekbones," Beau replied.

Maddie sighed. That compliment was actually kind of annoying. It's like he wasn't even listening to her. "No offense, but I wouldn't want to read a book about anyone's cheekbones. I prefer adventures, romances, fairy tales."

Beau grabbed Maddie's hands with his. "My fairy tale has already come true. I'm living it at this moment."

The door to the balcony opened, and a waiter came out with their food. "Pardon the interruption," he said.

"No, it's fine," Maddie assured him, letting go of Beau's hands. "What's your name? What's for dinner? What do you like to do for fun?" As hungry as she was for the meal, what she was really starved for was a good conversation.

As Beau's carriage drove across the countryside, Maddie couldn't help feeling disappointed in how her first date had gone. There were definitely no sparks or fireworks or anything like that. Most of the time she was with Beau, she had to fight just to stay awake.

For all she knew, though, maybe that's how dates normally were. She thought back to the story of *Beauty and the Beast*. It took months for Belle and the Beast to get to know each other and fall in love. Maybe she needed to spend a lot more time with Beau so that they could get to know each other.

Beau stopped the carriage outside Belle's cottage and jogged around the side to help her down. "My fair woman," he said, taking her by the hand, "words cannot convey the devastation I feel seeing this perfect evening come to an end."

"Yeah, okay, thanks," Maddie said. She took her hand back from him and hurried toward the front door of the house. "Bye!"

She was so relieved the date was over. It was only when she got inside that she remembered her plan to kiss Beau at the end of the date. Surprisingly, though, she wasn't sad that she missed her chance. What a disappointing first kiss that would have been. It's not like she would want to tell her grandkids someday about the time she kissed a guy who couldn't stop talking about her cheekbones. She would rather wait until she was on a date of her own, with a guy she actually liked, even if she had to wait a few more years.

She got the feeling Belle wouldn't have wanted to kiss Beau either. In fact, Belle would probably have preferred never to get married at all than to have a second date with someone like him. Beau was handsome, charming, and — she had to admit — kind of a dud. He didn't have any interest in getting to know Belle or, seemingly, anything interesting to say about himself either.

She thought it was going to be the best night of her life. Her first date . . . in a fairy tale! So why did it go so wrong? It didn't help that it took her so long to get ready, and then things only got worse when her date was so blinded by her looks that he couldn't look past them to see what was underneath.

Being beautiful was fun at first, but it was starting to look like it caused a whole lot of new problems.

Being in the fairy world hurt Holden's eyes. Everything was neon bright, like the store signs in the bad part of town. There were rainbows everywhere — not just in the sky but arcing over a cobblestone path and sprouting out of rabbit holes in the ground. There were beautiful trees with leaves that were orange, purple, and pink. Their trunks were full of knots that tiny glowing girls would pop in and out of, giggling as they flitted about like butterflies. Sugarplums dangled from branches like hanging fruit. Somewhere, an unseen flute was playing peppy music for everyone to hear.

No matter where Holden looked, he was assaulted by sunshine and cheer.

He felt like he might throw up.

It was almost as bad as a show choir concert, where all the dorky kids had fake smiles plastered on their faces as they harmonized on lame pop songs. At least he didn't have to go far to find Resplenda's home. He knew he was on the right track when he saw two very different men squeezing one after the other out of the tiny door to a cottage nestled among the trees.

"Oh, no! It's a stranger!" one of the men whimpered as he caught a glimpse of Holden. Squealing in fear, he sprinted away and took cover behind a bush.

The other guy marched right up to Holden. "Hey, watch this, pal," he boasted. He stepped back, crouched down, then sprung up and did three backflips down the path. "Ta-dah!" he announced with a flourish.

"Is he still here?" the man in the bush asked nervously, peering out from behind the leaves.

"Who are you two?" Holden asked.

The other man wrapped his arm around Holden and smiled proudly.

"Oh, you've probably read our story," he said. "*Shy Guy and the Showoff.*"

"Let me guess," Holden replied. "Cursed by Resplenda?"

"See, he's heard of her!" the Showoff said. "We're famous!"

"But I don't want to be famous!" the Shy Guy replied. "I want to be alone!"

"You got it," Holden said, walking past them both. "I don't have time for another messed-up spell. Good luck!"

He bent down by the tiny door he had seen the two men come through. "Hello?" He knocked. "I need to talk to you!"

"Certain as a curtain! Come in, pumpkin!" said a cheery voice.

Holden groaned. He hadn't even seen this fairy yet, and she was already annoying him. He crouched down as low as he could and squeezed through the door.

He'd never been in a fairy's home before, but it was pretty much as he would have expected. Everything was small, girly, and irritating, especially Resplenda herself. She was about eighteen inches tall, wore a fluffy pink dress, and buzzed around Holden's head in circles, checking him out.

"Funny, I don't remember cursing you!" she said. "What was your deal? Were you the Billionaire and the Bike Messenger guy? Soldier and the Scaredy Cat?"

"Beauty and the Beast," Holden said.

"Ooh, one of my favorites!" Resplenda chuckled. "But you don't look as beastly as I remember. Let me try again."

She circled his head, tossing pixie dust up in the air, and began a magical fairy chant. "Ugga-ugga-ugly! Ugga-ugga—"

"No! Stop!" Holden protested. "I'm not the Beast! It's this other dude, and trust me, you did a great job. He's a major monster."

"Oh, well three cheers for me! Hooray, hooray, hooray, hooray! I gave myself an extra cheer, 'cause I'm so great." Resplenda smiled. "Is that big baddie learning his lesson?"

"Well, no. All he's learning is that it sucks to be ugly. They arrested him, and they're going to execute him. He'll never get a fair trial looking the way he does. It's not right!"

"Oh boo-hoo," Resplenda taunted. "It's not right! Pity, pity, pity! Wah, wah, wah!"

"Don't mock me!" Holden said. "It's all because of your curse. It didn't make any sense. You took a shallow guy and made him gross, that much I get. But then you made it so that he could break the spell by marrying a total babe, so he was just as shallow as ever."

"Oh, foo!" Resplenda said, sticking her tongue out at him. "Do you always take the fun out of everything?"

"Kind of," Holden admitted. "But even fairy tales should follow some kind of logic."

"Wait a second, I know you!" Resplenda said. She whizzed about his head, checking him out. "Yes, of course! You're Sweetie Pie and the Snotface!"

"Sweetie Pie and the Snotface? What?" Holden said. "You know me?"

"Know you?" Resplenda laughed. "I cursed you! Why do you think you keep getting sucked into fairy tales? Ha, ha, ha!"

"So this is your fault?" Holden said. His face turned bright red in anger, and he started swatting at Resplenda with his hands. "You suck!" Every time he swiped at her, Resplenda quickly ducked out of the way. She was way too fast for him, and she seemed to enjoy his feeble attempts to catch her.

"Teeheehee!" she giggled. "La, la, la! I'm quicker than a snotface!"

Holden finally gave up. "Can you please just un-curse me? I'll stop making fun of fairy tales, I promise."

"Are you kidding?" Resplenda said. "This is too fun!"

Holden stood before her, stewing. "I hate fairy tales!" he screamed.

"But . . . ," she said, "I will do something for your friend, Mr. Beast. I'm nice! Yay for me!"

"You will?"

"Sure. He can be handsome again. Hunky, hunky, who'd'a thunky?"

"You're kidding! That's awesome!" Holden said.

"However . . . ," Resplenda added. "This woman he loves, Belle. I'm gonna have to take away her beauty. Bye-bye, Little Miss Cutie Pie!"

"What? Why would you do that?"

"The spell is Beauty and the Beast. Someone gets to be beautiful, but only if someone is a beast. Fair is fair!"

"I'll never convince her to give up her beauty. It's my sister, and she's having the time of her life putting on makeup and dating boys and all that gross stuff."

"Well, this might be a way to prove the Beast truly loves her. Like you said, he fell for a beauty — big deal. But if he can fall for a beast, he's really gone loco from the love bug!"

"Forget it. She won't do it."

"Well, whatever, whatever, just stay here forever!"

"Fine, I'll try!" Holden sighed.

"Good. Now be gone!" Resplenda replied. "You smell like boy! Phooey! Ptt! Ptt!"

She waved a magic wand, and in an instant, Holden was gone.

He found himself back at the law firm, sitting at his desk behind a mountain of files. It was late at night, and he was now only hours away from the start of his trial.

Somehow, between now and then, he had to convince his stepsister to become a monster.

Chapter
15

Maddie woke up with a puddle of drool on her pillow. She had never been a morning person, and it turned out being in a fairy tale didn't change that.

She was cranky, sluggish, and most of all, hungry. She could really go for a quiche like she had at the café yesterday. In fact, she felt like she could probably wolf down ten of them. She staggered to the kitchen to see what this cottage had to eat.

"Good morning, Belle!" said Belle's father. "How was your date last night?"

"Thumbs down!" Maddie said, frowning. "What a dud."

"I'm sorry to hear that. Here, maybe some porridge will cheer you up."

Porridge? People actually ate that? Maddie always thought it was something made up for *Goldilocks and the Three Bears*. Well, if it was good enough for Goldilocks, who was Maddie to complain?

Belle's dad pulled out a chair, and Maddie found herself sitting in front of a big, steaming bowl of . . . yuck! It looked like baby food: a big glop of lumpy tan mush in a bowl. It was so thick that her spoon stood straight up in the middle of it. As bad as it looked, it smelled even worse. She could barely stand to be near it, let alone eat it. It's not like she expected chocolate chip waffles for breakfast, but there was no way she was going to settle for this slop.

"Uh, no thanks," she said, pushing the bowl away.

"You seem to be very choosy lately," said a voice from behind her. Maddie turned around and saw Jeanette sitting in the next room. "First with your date, now with your breakfast. Care to talk about it?" She waved her hand toward the fainting couch, inviting Maddie to have a seat.

Maddie glared at Belle's father. "You brought the therapist back?"

"You seemed so unhappy when you got home last night," he explained. "Just go sit with her for a minute."

"Actually, I feel like taking a walk," Maddie said. "I'm going to go into town to score some quiche."

"Heavens, no!" he replied. "You can't go into town looking like that!"

"Like what?"

"Here, take a look," Belle's dad said. He took a small mirror off the wall and showed it to her.

"Aah!" Maddie screamed when she saw her reflection. There was smeared makeup all over her cheeks and bags underneath her eyes. Tiny hairs sprouted above her upper lip and on her chin, and she had a major case of bed head. Maddie thought back to the time Holden took the picture of her in the morning and Instagrammed it so the whole school could see. At least there was no social media in fairy tales. Still, though, she definitely needed to freshen up before going out in public.

"Thanks for the heads-up," she said to Belle's father. "I guess even Belle can have morning face."

"You mean you?" Jeanette replied.

"Huh?"

"You called yourself Belle again. You do know you're Belle, right?"

"Ugh, I need to get out of here!" Maddie groaned.

She bent over the sink and began to wash her makeup off. After splashing water on herself for a minute, she checked the mirror. Much better. She didn't have time to do her hair, so she pulled it back and grabbed a hat from the coat closet.

"Okay, see ya!" she said. "Want me to bring you back anything from the café?"

Belle's father chuckled. "Very funny, Belle. You know you can't leave the house looking like that."

"What do you mean?" Maddie asked. "I'm okay now."

"You haven't done your hair or your makeup. You haven't taken a bath or put on one of your beautiful dresses."

"Belle does that every day?" She glanced over and saw Jeanette shaking her head and writing on her notepad. "I mean, I do? Me? Belle? I do that every day?"

"Of course. A lady needs to make herself presentable. That's why you never leave the house before noon!" Belle's father said.

"Noon?!" It wasn't even nine o'clock.

Maddie wanted to stick to Belle's routine, but there was no way she was going to waste her entire morning making herself look better just so she could go out for breakfast. "I'm sorry," she said, "but I need to eat something before I can even think of spending three hours primping. Later!"

Belle's father gasped, but Maddie didn't care that she didn't look perfect. She was just dreaming of that quiche.

As Maddie stepped outside, she heard Belle's father lament, "Why can't I get through to her?"

"That Beast really messed with her head," Jeanette said.

When Maddie reached the village, she saw some of the same people who greeted her so warmly yesterday. "Hi there!" she waved to the glass blower.

"Oh . . . well . . . hello," he replied. He seemed awkward and uncomfortable, and he quickly returned to his work.

Other people reacted just as strangely. Instead of greeting her, some people just pointed at her and whispered to their friends.

"Belle? Are you okay?" one woman asked.

"I'm fine," Maddie said as cheerily as possible. The woman shrugged and walked away.

Maddie didn't understand why people's reactions were so different than they were yesterday. She couldn't wait to get to Café LeGrande. She knew the baker would be nicer to her.

"Good morning!" Maddie said as she entered the café. No one replied. Everyone just stared.

"Belle?" the baker poked his head out from the kitchen. "What happened to you?"

"What do you mean?" Maddie asked. "Nothing happened."

"It's just that . . . never mind," he said.

"I've been dreaming of your delicious quiche. Did I tell you how absolutely marvelous it was?"

"Oh, very nice," the baker replied. "I'll get you one."

"Thanks. I'll wait out front," Maddie said.

"No," the baker replied. "Please, wait over there." He pointed to a corner where no one was sitting, and then went back into the kitchen.

Maddie sat at the empty table, sulking. Everyone was acting so differently today.

"Oh no," said a man. "Aren't you usually pretty?"

"Excuse me?" Maddie replied.

"You're that lady everyone thinks is so pretty. Why do you look like you got trampled on by a goat?"

"Monsieur Voltaire!" said a waiter. He ran up and tried to shoo the man away. "Please leave her alone."

"No, wait," Maddie said, turning to the man. "I want to talk to you. Please sit down."

Monsieur Voltaire sat down across from Maddie while she waited for her quiche. "Is this a shoe store?" he asked.

"No, it's a café. Just tell me, is it true that people are nicer to you when you're good-looking?"

"Well, of course," he said. "Even I know that."

Maddie hung her head sadly. No wonder Belle spent so long getting ready every day. People expected it of her. She never realized being beautiful could be such a burden. At that moment, the baker emerged with her quiche. He set it down in front of her with a quick, "Here you go!" then started to walk away.

"What's this?" Maddie asked, picking up a small slip of paper that was tucked under the plate.

"That's your bill," the baker said.

Maddie sighed. Monsieur Voltaire was salivating over her food. "Are you going to eat that steak?"

"It's a quiche," Maddie replied glumly, "and you can have it."

She stood up to leave the café. All of a sudden, she had lost her appetite.

Chapter 16

Holden stared out his office window, wondering how he would ever get Maddie to agree to become a beast. Being Belle was like a dream come true for her. She probably spent all her time looking at herself in the mirror, trying on different outfits, and kissing napkins with her lipstick. Those seemed like the kinds of things pretty girls probably did all day.

As he watched the villagers go by, he noticed an annoyed-looking woman coming out of the café. She was a total mess. Her hair was pulled back and tucked into a hat. Her skin was saggy, and she looked tired. She was wearing baggy pants and a plain blue shirt. She looked almost as bad as Maddie did that time he Instagrammed a picture of her morning face.

Then, Holden took a closer look at the woman. Was that . . . ? He sprang from his desk and ran out of the office.

"Maddie!" he shouted across the street. "Maddie!"

"What?" Maddie asked defiantly.

He crossed the street and met up with her on the corner. "Um, why do you look like you got hit by a truck?"

"So what if I do!" Maddie shouted. "Who says you have to look perfect all the time? This is what Belle looks like in the morning, and I think she's still beautiful. She shouldn't have to spend all day making herself up just to impress everyone!"

"Whoa," Holden responded, "even in fairy tales, you're not a morning person."

Maddie sighed. "I shouldn't take it out on you. I just feel bad for Belle. Being beautiful is a lot of work. And for what? You can never tell if people really like you for who you are or if they just think you're pretty."

"Sounds like you're having as lousy a time in this fairy tale as I am. I found a way to make the Beast handsome, but—" He stopped short, thinking about what she had just said. "Did you say you're sick of being beautiful?"

"Why?" Maddie asked him, suspiciously.

Holden smiled. "Come on!" He grabbed her by the arm and started to lead her down the street.

"This place is creepy," Maddie said, as Holden led her into a dark, misty forest. "Where are you taking me?"

"Quiet," Holden replied. "I'm trying to count. Eighty-one . . . eighty-two . . ." Maddie sighed, unsure why she was following him. All she knew was that she had no clue how to give Belle back her happily ever after, and if Holden had an idea, she was willing to see what it was. Soon, they came to a winding river, and Holden stopped.

That's when Maddie noticed something very strange about this river. There was a small section of it, right in front of them, that ran backward, against the rest of the river's current. "How strange," she marveled. "Why is it doing that?"

"Fairy tales are full of weird stuff," Holden said. "I'm over it." With that, he yanked her by the arm into the current.

"Hey! Holden! I'm getting wet!"

"You'll dry off at Resplenda's house," he assured her.

"What? Who's Resplenda?"

"Not now," Holden said, deep in thought. "I have to think of an impossible wish."

Maddie huffed, yanking her arm away from him. "I wish you would just give me a straight answer for once!"

There was a great rumble, followed by a flash of light. Maddie watched in awe as a door appeared on the opposite bank of the river.

"Nice one!" Holden said, and together they began to wade through the river toward the door.

Maddie wasn't even sure what she had done, but she followed Holden through the door, eager to see what lay on the other side.

Maddie stepped wide-eyed into the fairy world, gazing around her in awe. She gaped at the giggling fairies flitting around like fireflies. She did a double take as a rainbow sprouted up just a few feet in front of her, arcing across the sky as if by magic.

"Wow!" she said.

"Figures you'd like this dump," Holden said. He swatted at a passing fairy as if she were a gnat. "Come on, let's go see Resplenda."

Maddie followed Holden to the door of a small cottage. As they bent down, they could hear voices arguing inside. Holden didn't even bother to knock. He just turned the knob and threw the door open. "Holden, you can't just barge into somebody's house!" Maddie protested.

"It's okay," Holden assured her. "She knows us."

Maddie followed Holden inside. She suddenly felt as though she was standing in her dollhouse from when she was little. Everything was adorably miniature-sized, including a doll-sized fairy that buzzed around the two men she was talking to. One of the men wore a fancy suit with gold cufflinks. The other wore bicycle pants and had a messenger bag slung over his shoulder. That man was pleading with the fairy.

"I've learned my lesson," he begged. "Can I please have all my money back?"

Holden leaned into Maddie and whispered in her ear. "This must be the Billionaire and the Bike Messenger."

"The what and the who?" she replied.

"That guy was a rich jerk, so the fairy cursed them and made them switch places."

Resplenda shook her head defiantly. "You can't break the spell until you find true love. First the honey, then the money! Teeheehee!" She tossed a wad of fairy dust gleefully into the air.

Maddie was starting to catch on. She leaned in and whispered to Holden. "So that other guy was poor, and now he's rich?" Holden nodded.

The man in the fancy suit smiled excitedly, bowing down to Resplenda. "Thank you so much! I love this curse!"

Resplenda shooed the two men away. "I'm bored with you! Off you go! Ta-ta! Toodle-oodle! Time to skedoodle!"

She used her fairy magic to open the door for the men. As they left the cottage, Holden led Maddie forward to talk to Resplenda.

"Is this who I think it is?" Maddie whispered. "Is this the same fairy who cursed the Beast?"

"Duh," Holden said. "Didn't I explain that?"

"Well, hi, hi, hi!" Resplenda giggled, circling around Maddie's head. "It's that obnoxious guy, and a sweetie pie! Guess she's ready to uglify?"

"Huh? What is she talking about?" Maddie asked.

"Well, you said you were tired of being beautiful, right?" Holden said. "Great news! Resplenda is going to curse you!"

"What? I don't want to be cursed!"

"Oh, come on! You didn't explain this to her?" Resplenda said, shooting fairy dust in Holden's face. "Once a snotface, always a snotface!"

"Snotface?" Maddie repeated, curiously. "Where have I heard that before?" Maddie thought the odd word sounded very familiar, but she couldn't recall who had said it to her recently.

Holden sighed, realizing it was time to tell Maddie what he'd learned. "Resplenda is not just the one who cursed the Beast," he explained. "She also cursed us. That's why we're in this fairy tale."

"Really?" Maddie said, turning toward Resplenda, her expression hard to read.

The fairy trembled nervously as Maddie stepped toward her. "Um . . . yeah, kinda, I guess maybe I sorta, you know . . ."

"Thank you so much!" Maddie gushed. She reached out and shook Resplenda's hand. "This is really cool! Can we do Rapunzel next? I've always loved her hair!"

"Sorry, I don't take requests, honey," Resplenda said.

"Focus, Maddie," Holden scolded. "Resplenda's going to give Beast back his old face so he'll be handsome again, and in return she'll make Belle a hideous freak. Then once he falls in love with you as a monster, it'll prove he's not shallow, and the curse will be broken."

"But what if he doesn't love me once I'm no longer beautiful?"

Resplenda shrugged. "Then he'll pick up some hot little dish and you'll be stuck here as a beast forever."

"Forever?"

"Forever and ever and ever!" Resplenda chuckled. "Infinity-times-infinity years. Till the sun don't shine, the end of time!"

Maddie took a deep breath and thought over the difficult choice in front of her. She had seen how people behaved toward Belle when she was beautiful, and how they weren't as kind when she wasn't. What would happen when she was ugly? Would anyone be able to see that Belle was still the same kind, thoughtful person she had always been? Would the Beast? If he truly loved her, then he wouldn't care how she looked, but that was a big gamble to take.

"It all comes down to one thing," Resplenda said. "Do you believe in true love, sweetie?"

That settled it. If there was one thing in the world Maddie believed in, it was true love. She saw it with her father and Carol, and she was willing to bet everything that it existed with Belle and the Beast, too. "Let's do it," Maddie replied confidently.

"Really?" Holden asked. "You know you're going to be even grosser-looking than usual."

"Ha, ha," Maddie told him. "Go ahead, Resplenda. Make me a beast."

Resplenda smiled. "Magica, magica! Bing, bang, zow!" she said, and she began casting huge waves of fairy dust in Maddie's direction. The sparkling dust swirled around her, covering her face. "Make this sweetie pie ugly now!"

Holden watched in awe as Maddie transformed before his eyes. Her arms became furry, and her hands grew sharp claws. Her face was still covered by fairy dust, but as it began to settle, he could almost make out what she had become.

"Whoa . . ." was all he could say in response.

Maddie swallowed nervously, wondering if she had made the right choice.

Chapter 17

When Maddie had discovered her first pimple, it felt like the end of the world. She spent an hour staring at it in the mirror, in all its red, pukey disgustingness. It had popped up out of nowhere on the most obvious place on her face, the very tip of her nose. She felt like Rudolph the Red-Nosed Loser. All that morning, she tried everything she could think of to cover it up, or at least make it less noticeable. Lotions only made it shinier. Popping it only made it oozier. She finally realized that if she kept her head bowed, her bangs cast a slight shadow over her face, so she walked around all day as if she were staring at something on the ground. More people asked her if something was wrong with her neck than they did about the zit. Still, it was horrible, humiliating, the worst day of her life.

Being a beast was like that, times a billion. The only bright side was that there was no way Jake Templeton was going to see her here.

Instead, she had to face the townspeople in Belle's village. She thought back to how horribly they reacted when she showed up with morning face. She didn't just have morning face now. She had morning body, morning claws, morning tusks. Every part of her was hairy, misshapen, and foul. She had pointed ears and long fangs, a hunch in her back, and whiskers jutting out from her nose.

"I don't think I should go into town like this," she confessed as she and Holden approached the village.

"Honestly," Holden assured her, "I can barely tell the difference between this and your old face." He cackled at his joke.

Maddie let out a fearsome growl and bared her Wolverine-like claws. She wasn't even aware she was doing it at first, but it was fierce, and Holden cowered in response.

"Whoa, I take it back," he said meekly.

For the first time since her transformation, Maddie smiled. "I didn't know I could do that. I guess there are good things about being a beast."

"I have an idea," Holden said. "We'll sneak you in."

"All the way across town? How?"

Holden patted her back reassuringly. "Just follow me."

He led Maddie into the village through a back alley. They crouched underneath windows so they wouldn't be seen. When they came to a street, he checked to make sure no one was looking, and then he waved for her to come out. She hurried across the street, until she heard a man coming out of a nearby shop.

"Duck under the apple cart!" Holden instructed. Maddie dove for cover, getting out of sight just in time. Underneath the cart, Maddie laid perfectly still and watched as the man casually sauntered past. Once he was far away, Holden waved for Maddie to emerge. She stood up and brushed herself off, and then followed Holden to a trellis.

"What are you doing?" she asked him.

"Come on," he said, climbing up the side of the building. "No one will see us up here!"

She followed him up, and from there, they jumped from one rooftop to the next. It was bold and daring, completely unlike anything Maddie would normally do. But she felt totally at ease, able to creep, prowl, and leap like a wild animal. It was kind of exciting.

They passed right over a crowded marketplace without being spotted, and soon the jail was within sight.

Maddie couldn't help being impressed by her stepbrother's skills of evasion. "How did you get so good at this?" she asked.

"What do you think I do when I'm late to school?" he said, smiling proudly. "Never got detention once."

He jumped off the roof and landed in a bale of hay below.

"I'm not jumping from up here!" Maddie said, peering over the edge of the building.

"Why? Afraid you'll ruin your good looks?"

"I'll get you for that!" Maddie growled. She closed her eyes and leapt off the roof into the hay. It was a hard fall, but she had such a big, sturdy body that she was able to get right up again. Another plus for beastliness.

They were just around the corner from the jail now, and Maddie got struck with another case of nerves. "Wait, I can't see him like this. He's going to be handsome. What if I get nervous or tongue-tied?" She thought about how she sometimes was around Jake Templeton. She would get so jittery she could barely remember her name.

Holden laughed. "I'd be more worried about how he's going to react, if I were you. At least he can't run away." Holden opened the jailhouse door for Maddie and followed her inside.

The room they found themselves in was dim, lit only by candles. They smelled fresh strawberries and delicious baked goods. Nearby, a woman softly sang a love song in French. It was hardly anything like the jail. It was more like the ladies' underwear store at the mall.

"Are we in the right place?" Maddie asked.

A beautiful woman swept into the room. She wore a flowing dress. Her hair was long and silky, and she sang with the sweet voice of a nightingale.

"Yo, who's that babe?" Holden whispered.

Maddie stared at the woman, wondering the same thing. What could someone so glamorous possibly be doing in the jailhouse? As the woman picked up two plates full of food, Maddie heard a jingling sound coming from her hip. There was a ring of keys dangling from her side.

Maddie took another look at the woman's face and gasped in shock. "It's Simone!"

"Whoa, who put a spell on her and made her so glam?" Holden asked.

"I think she did it herself," Maddie replied. "She must've spent hours getting ready today."

"Why would she suddenly care how she looks?"

Maddie peered down the hallway and caught a glimpse of the Beast in his cell. He was tall and tan, with dark hair that swooped neatly across his forehead. He had perfect skin, brilliant blue eyes, and rippling muscles that, if not for a fairy's magic spell, he would have had to spend eons in the gym to achieve. He looked like the kind of man who could appear in a black and white perfume ad, lying shirtless on the beach as a wave crashed over his feet.

Maddie's stomach dropped as she realized what was going on. "She likes him," she said. "Now that he's handsome, she likes him."

"Huh?" Holden asked. "How can you tell?"

Maddie rolled her eyes. "Duh, why else would she get all dressed up?"

Boys could be so clueless sometimes.

"Who do I hear?" Simone asked. She held up a candle and gazed toward the doorway, at Maddie and Holden. "Aah!" she screamed, marching toward them. "Who is that monster?"

"I'm here to see the Beast," Maddie said.

Simone laughed cruelly. "Maybe you should look in a mirror."

"You know who she means," Holden said. "Mesher de What's-His-Face."

Simone curled her lip. "I'll tell him you're here."

"Maybe I should come with you," Holden said. "Don't worry," he told Maddie. "I'll get you in."

Holden followed Simone down the hallway. He hadn't taken a good look at the Beast yet, and when he saw him, he was taken aback. "Whoa! Hunk alert!"

"Isn't he the handsomest man you've ever seen?" Simone asked flirtatiously. The Beast blushed.

Holden nodded, impressed. "Let's just say if you went to my school, your name would be written in a lot of girls' notebooks."

"I don't know what happened," the Beast confessed. "I was sitting down, preparing my final words for when I'm executed tonight, and all of a sudden, this swirling, glowing dust cloud appeared. It swept me off my feet and turned me around, and when it put me back down, I looked like my old self again. My body, my face, everything was just as it used to be. I think the curse was broken!"

"Well, that's part of it," Holden said.

"What do you mean?" the Beast asked.

"There's someone here to see you," Holden replied. "I'll let her tell you." Holden walked back down the hall to get Maddie, leaving Simone alone with the Beast.

"Who is it?" the Beast asked. "Who's here?"

"Some horrid-looking woman," Simone snarled. "Do you want to see her? Or would you rather be alone with me and have some of this strawberry crêpe I made you?" She picked up a crêpe and dipped it in chocolate sauce. Then, she dangled it just inches from his face. He stared at the treat, practically drooling.

"I thought prisoners weren't allowed to have desserts," he replied.

"Well, I didn't think prisoners could be so handsome!" Simone said, popping a bit of the crêpe in his mouth.

As Holden returned to Maddie, he looked over his shoulder to see what was happening. He watched as the Beast took a long bite of the crêpe, savoring the taste, then licked every drop of chocolate off his lips. Holden shook his head and turned to Maddie. "Whoa, he likes her, too."

"How can you tell?" Maddie asked.

This time, Holden rolled his eyes at her. "Duh. Why else would he eat French food?"

The Beast went to take another bite of the crêpe. But just as he opened his mouth, Simone pulled the treat away.

"Do you want some more?" she asked him. "I'd be happy to stay and feed you the whole thing."

"Oh yes, please!" the Beast said, salivating.

"Very well," Simone said. "I will get rid of that horrid she-beast at once!"

"Do it!" the Beast said, taking the rest of the crêpe from her. Simone laughed heartily as he devoured it whole.

"Whoa," Holden said. "That was pretty harsh."

He turned toward Maddie to see how she was handling this, only to discover that she was no longer standing beside him. Instead, he found the jailhouse door standing ajar. Maddie had run away.

Holden couldn't believe it, but he actually felt bad for his stepsister.

Chapter 18

Maddie fled into the street. She couldn't bear to watch the Beast and Simone flirting anymore. Could it be that as soon as the Beast became handsome he forgot about Belle and all she meant to him? Would he really ditch her for the first pretty woman who showed interest in him? Had the fairy tale she had believed in been a lie all along?

She was in such a hurry to get out of the jailhouse that she forgot what she now looked like. As she wandered through town, people began to point at her and gasp. A few screamed in horror. Children ran away in fear.

"It's a new beast!" one man shouted.

"Stay away from my children!" wailed a panicked woman.

Maddie gazed around her. Everyone was staring at her. People came out of their shops and stuck their heads out of the windows of their homes for a better look.

"No, I'm not a monster!" she explained. "I'm—"

"Get out of our town!" yelled the baker.

The same man who had been so nice to her when she was beautiful was now suddenly so cruel.

Maddie's heart pounded, as dozens of angry villagers circled around her with fear and anger in their faces. They were all shouting at once, so much that she could only catch a few words here and there. "Animal!" "Barbarian!" "Attack!" She felt scared, overwhelmed. There was no telling what they might do.

And then, before she knew what she was doing, Maddie bared her claws and let out a mighty roar.

"RWWWAAAARRRRRRRRRRR!!!"

The sound was so tremendous it shook the rafters of the buildings. It drowned out the clamor of the angry mob. What followed it was a sheer, chilly silence. Everyone backed away from Maddie in absolute terror. They held their breath to see what she might do.

"Don't hurt us!" someone whimpered.

Maddie felt such a mix of emotions. She felt rage at how they intimidated her, but also guilt for the way she scared them in return. This was what being a beast was like. This was what she had foolishly allowed herself to be turned into. This, she feared, was what she was now doomed to be forever.

And then, a single voice cried out from across the street. "Belle?" it said uncertainly.

Everyone looked to see who had made the outrageous claim. The crowd parted, and an old man came into view.

"Belle!" he cried. "It is you!"

It was Belle's father. He ran through the crowd and drew Maddie into his arms, hugging her tightly.

"How did you know it was me?" Maddie asked him. "I look so different."

"You're my little girl, Belle. I don't just see you with my eyes," he said. "I see you with my heart."

He held her and let her cry into his shoulder. Maddie's thoughts wandered to her own father and the love he always showed for her when she was feeling low. The morning she found the zit, he pretended like he couldn't see it. He even took out a magnifying glass, trying to convince her it was so small it couldn't be seen with the naked eye. She had no doubt her father would hold her exactly like this if she ever turned into a beast.

"Oh my dear!" Belle's father said. "Who did this to you?"

"I did it to myself," Maddie replied. "I wanted to see if anyone could still love me as a beast."

"Love you? My sweet Belle, I will always love you!"

"I love you, too, Daddy!" Maddie said.

The townspeople watched in confusion, shocked that the monster they had been crowding around was actually their beloved Belle. Some of them began to cry.

"You should be ashamed!" Belle's father said to them. "You mock her because she's ugly, but no one has a more beautiful heart! Come, Belle," he told her. "Let's go home."

Once again, the villagers parted to allow Belle and her father to pass through.

"We're sorry, Belle," the baker said.

"Will you be coming to the Beast's trial?" a woman asked.

Maddie sighed. She had a lot to think about. "I'm not sure," she said. Then she and Belle's father continued walking down the road and out of the village.

Chapter 19

Holden pinched himself in the arm, hard enough to make it hurt. Then, he counted to five. Then, he pinched himself again, a little bit harder. He kept doing this, over and over, because it was the only way he could think of to keep himself awake during the Beast's trial. Court was so boring!

It turned out real trials weren't nearly as fun as the ones on TV. Sure, the courtroom was packed with villagers, and yes, a gasp went up when they all saw the Beast's handsome new appearance. But there wasn't a lot of shouting going on or surprise witnesses or people being held in contempt.

So far, it had just been a prosecutor laying out evidence and random losers going on and on about stuff that barely mattered. One of the Beast's gardeners told the court what he saw the day Belle first arrived at the castle. A housekeeper described the room in which Belle was kept. She called it a "cell," and Holden rose up, shouting and pointing his finger at her accusingly.

"Objection!" he thundered. "It wasn't a cell! It was just a room in his castle!"

"Okay, okay," the judge said. "You don't have to shout."

Holden sighed and sat back down. Even the fun stuff wasn't as fun as he thought it would be.

The prosecutor's star witness was a therapist. Some lady named Jeanette. She took the stand and held up a notebook. "I've been observing Belle since she returned from her captivity. I made a note every time she did something I found odd." She flipped through the notebook, showing that every page was full of writing.

"And you think this was related to her time with the defendant?"

"Absolutely," Jeanette replied. "It's a natural progression. First, she was afraid of her captor. Then, she sympathized with him. Finally, she fell in love with him. It's classic behavior for a kidnap victim."

"Is there a name for this condition?" the lawyer asked.

Jeanette nodded. "Personally, I call it Kidnap-Victim-Falling-For-Captor-Syndrome."

"Objection!" Holden said, then he added softly, "It's called Stockholm Syndrome." He hated agreeing with her, but he'd been saying this about Belle since the beginning, and he wanted them to at least get the name of the condition right.

As the trial continued, Holden kept one eye on the courtroom door, hoping Maddie would show up. By now, he wasn't very optimistic. Maybe his stepsister had given up hope of going home and was willing to stay in this twisted fairy tale with a beast face forever. Well, he didn't want to be stuck here even one more day. He realized he was going to have to win this case without her.

"Monsieur Rousseau . . . Monsieur Rousseau. . ."

It didn't help that Holden still had trouble recognizing his own name. "Oh right!" he said, snapping to attention. "That's me. What's up?"

"The prosecution has rested," the judge sighed. "You may call your first witness."

"Oh cool. In that case, I call to the stand, the prisoner formerly known as the Beast!"

The Beast quietly took the stand. While he was sworn in, Holden flipped through the files laid out in front of him on the defense desk, trying to figure out the first question he should ask.

That's when he remembered that everything was written in French. He was going to have to wing it.

The entire courtroom turned toward Holden, anxious to see what course his defense would take. Knowing he had their full attention, Holden stood up and took a dramatic pause. A very long pause. People leaned forward in their seats to hear what he would say.

But instead of speaking, Holden just started to nod. Nod and walk. He silently paced back and forth in front of the witness stand. Every eye followed him, thinking this was some brilliant legal tactic. Really, though, he just couldn't think of anything to say.

Finally, it came to him. The perfect question to open with. As everyone listened closely, he turned toward the Beast and asked him.

"So did you kidnap her or what?"

The Beast looked directly at the judge and nodded his head. "Yes," he said. "I did."

The crowd let out a collective gasp. Holden's jaw dropped. He was just as shocked as anyone else in the room. "Your Honor, can I have a minute to see if my client has gone loony?"

The judge banged his gavel. "Oh, come on. Let him talk," he said.

The Beast sat up straight in his chair, held his head high, and spoke from his heart. "Your Honor, I am guilty. I held a woman in my castle against her will. I was cruel and angry. I yelled at her. I told her she could never leave. I was exactly what everyone has been saying I was: a beast."

More gasps went up from the crowd. Finally, this trial was getting interesting, but not in the way Holden had hoped. If the Beast kept talking like this, he would face the guillotine for sure.

"Hold on," Holden said. "If you were so mean to Belle, then why would she want to marry you?"

"Well, I wasn't always mean. After I got to know her, I calmed down."

"Aha!" Holden said. He thought back to everything he knew about the story. "Didn't you make her nice dinners? Give her fancy dresses to wear? Dance with her like people do at weddings and stuff?"

"Yes, I did all those things."

"You sound like a pretty decent dude to me. And didn't you let her go home to see her dad once?" Holden vaguely remembered a part of the story when Belle asked if she could go home to check on her father's health.

"I did."

"Okay, well if she was being held captive, then as soon as you let her go, she probably would've run to the police to report you. Is that what she did?"

"No. She checked on her father, and then she returned to me."

"She returned? By herself? No cops?"

The Beast shook his head. Holden smiled. He felt like he was on a roll, leading the Beast exactly where he wanted him to go. This is how TV lawyers did it. He started thinking he should totally become an actor when he grew up so he could play lawyer characters. He'd be so good at it. "So you're saying she could come and go from the castle? And when she left, she came back even though she didn't have to?"

"Well, yes," the Beast agreed.

"Doesn't sound to me like she was your prisoner." Holden saw the judge nodding along. He had convinced him, he was sure of it. Now was the perfect time to whip out another TV lawyer catch phrase. "Your Honor," he said. "I rest my case!"

Holden held up his hand as if he were holding a microphone, and then pretended to drop it. "Mic drop!" He smirked, then proudly strutted back to his seat, gloating at the prosecutor.

The prosecutor seemed taken aback by Holden's expression. He didn't seem flustered at all by the questions, though. He calmly stood up and addressed the judge. "Your Honor, I'd like to cross-examine the witness."

"What?!" Holden said. "He can't do that!"

"Well, sure he can," the judge said.

"But I dropped the mic!"

"You did what?" the judge asked, puzzled. "Who's Mike?"

Holden groaned. "Darn it!" he shouted. He folded his arms angrily across his chest.

"Just one thing," the prosecutor said to the Beast. "When you took this woman as your prisoner, were you under a spell?"

"Well, yes. I was."

"And did you need a woman to fall in love with you in order to break the spell?"

"Yes."

"So you needed Belle to fall in love with you. Isn't that why you started being nice to her?"

"No, she taught me to love. I really cared for her!"

"Of course you did," the prosecutor said sarcastically. "And now that the spell has been broken, she wouldn't even come to court to support you."

"Objection!" Holden shouted. Everyone in the courtroom looked at him, but he had nothing else to say.

"Why are you objecting?" the judge asked.

Holden searched his brain for any other phrase he could remember from TV shows. Badgering? No, that didn't sound right. Asked and answered? No, probably not. "Um . . . leading the witness!" he said.

The judge nodded thoughtfully. "Yeah, okay. Sustained," he said.

"Yes!" Holden shouted, pumping his fist in the air.

"Withdrawn," the prosecutor said, unconcerned. "Nothing further," he added. As he sat back down, he looked over at Holden and smirked, making the same gloating face Holden had made at him a few minutes ago.

"I take it back!" Holden said, standing up. "I don't rest my case!"

"Very well," the judge said. "Then who's your next witness?"

"My next witness?"

"You have to call a witness or rest your case. Those are the only two choices."

"My next witness . . . my next witness . . . " Holden scanned the courtroom, knowing he'd reached a dead end. He had done his best, but he couldn't think of anything else that could possibly save the Beast at this point. He opened his mouth to tell the judge that he was done.

But at just that moment, the courtroom door opened. Every head turned, and everyone gasped at what they saw.

Everyone, that is, except Holden. When he saw who was standing there, he smiled.

"My next witness," he said, "is Belle!"

Even the judge gasped now. Holden couldn't be more psyched. This was just the kind of shocking twist that always went over huge on TV!

Chapter
20

Maddie took a deep breath as she entered the courtroom. She had spent all afternoon debating whether to show up for the trial. She knew people would point and stare at her the way they did in the village, and she wasn't sure she could stand to go through that again. Then she thought about how Belle's father recognized her when no one else did. His love for her allowed him to see that what looked like a monster was really his beloved daughter. If the Beast loved her, perhaps he, too, would be able to see beyond her appearance.

"Belle?" the Beast cried out as she took the witness stand. Maddie gazed at him, and for a moment their eyes met. She searched his face to see what he was feeling, but all she saw was a look of horror. Maddie wasn't quite sure what that meant.

Holden was stoked. He pumped his fist, savoring the excitement in the room. Everyone was gawking at Belle's beastly face. He didn't need to pinch himself anymore to stay awake. Sparks were about to fly at this trial! "Would you state your name for the record, Maddie?" he asked.

The spectators were abuzz. *What did he call her?*

"I mean, ma'am," Holden corrected himself.

"I'm Belle," Maddie replied.

"Belle?" Holden pretended to be shocked. "But Belle is the most beautiful woman in all of France. No offense, lady, but you're kind of a mess."

Maddie rolled her eyes. Holden could be so harsh. "I was cursed by a fairy," she explained. "That's why I look like this."

"No!" the Beast cried out.

"I'm as shocked as you are!" the judge said to the Beast.

"Hold on," Holden said, acting confused. "I thought the defendant was the one who was cursed by a fairy."

"He was," Maddie said, "but I had the fairy reverse the curse and make me the ugly one."

"Belle!" the Beast cried out, rising from his seat. "No!"

The judge banged his gavel. "Please, sit back down. I need to hear the rest of this. Oh, I'm dying up here!" The Beast reluctantly sat. The judge leaned forward on the bench, riveted.

"Why would you agree to give up your beauty?" Holden asked.

"Because I knew he wouldn't get a fair trial looking the way he did."

Maddie stared into the Beast's eyes, and she could see that behind his handsome exterior, he was still the same man. The way he looked at her. The kindness in his soul. He began to cry. "Why are you crying?" Maddie asked him. "Is it because of how hideous I look?"

"No," the Beast replied, wiping away his tears. "It's because I've never felt so loved."

Maddie began to cry as well. The horror was gone from the Beast's face. Now when she looked into his eyes, all she saw was love.

"My dear, sweet Belle," the Beast said, rising from his seat.

"Monsieur de Maupassant," the judge scolded, "You're not supposed to stand up yet!"

The Beast ignored his plea, walking toward Belle with his hand extended.

"Monsieur de Maupassant!"

"Belle, to me you are every bit as beautiful now as you were the day you came to my castle," the Beast said, taking

Belle's hand. "They can lock me in jail, they can send me to my death, but I will never stop loving you. Will you do me the honor of being my wife?"

Maddie began to giggle. She couldn't help it. She had always wondered what it would be like when a man proposed marriage to her. Now that it had happened, it was every bit as magical as she had always hoped. Of course, this was Belle's proposal, not hers, but she felt confident she knew how Belle would respond.

"Yes!" Maddie said. "I'd love to!"

Holden looked to see if the judge was still upset, but by now, he was wiping away tears of his own. "That was beautiful!" he cried.

There wasn't a dry eye in the entire courtroom, except Holden's. He found the whole thing a little corny. He also thought it was a great opportunity to wrap things up. "So is my client free to go?" Holden asked.

"Oh I almost forgot," the judge said. "I still need to rule. Silly me! Just a formality. Gotta do it."

Holden gave Maddie a thumbs-up. He could sense that they'd be on their way back home any second.

"Can everyone please take their seats?" the judge said.

Maddie stepped down from the witness stand and took a seat in the courtroom. The Beast returned to the defense table, and Holden gave him a fist bump. "Dude, you got this!" he whispered.

"In the matter of the People versus the Beast," the judge said, raising his gavel, "on the charge of kidnapping, I find the Beast . . ." He took a long pause. Holden turned around to Maddie and winked at her confidently.

"GUILTY!" the judge bellowed, slamming his gavel down.

Chapter 21

"Are you nuts?" Holden yelled. The entire courtroom was in an uproar over the judge's ruling. Everyone had thought for sure after the show of emotion between Belle and the Beast that the Beast would be set free. No one could believe that the judge had declared him guilty.

"Order!" the judge shouted, banging his gavel. "Order!" He waited for everyone to calm down before explaining his ruling. "After listening to the testimony, I do believe the Beast is guilty of kidnapping Belle. However, this man sitting at the defense table is not the Beast."

The spectators murmured in confusion, unsure what the judge meant.

"This experience changed him, and he's no longer the man who held Belle against her will. He's kind and loving and true, and if she has forgiven him, that's good enough for me, too. I hereby order the defendant released!"

A cheer rose up from the crowd.

The Beast ran to Maddie and gave her a hug. "Furthermore," the judge said, "I order the curse undone."

"What?" Maddie said. "You can do that?"

"Well, I can't," said the judge. Suddenly a huge cloud of smoke rose up around the judge and a flash of light illuminated the room. The cloud dissipated in a sprinkle of fairy dust, and standing in the middle was Resplenda.

"But I can!" she said.

Holden was stunned. "Resplenda? You were the judge?"

"Woohoohoo! I tricked you!" Resplenda flitted around the upper reaches of the courtroom, to the amazement of everyone watching.

"Does this mean you'll make Belle a babe again?" Holden asked.

"No no, no can do," Resplenda said. "Two beauties is beyond my duty! But I can cast a swell new spell! Easy peasy fridge and freezy!"

"What will that do?" Maddie asked.

"Just tell us without the rhymes, please," Holden begged.

"Well, I can't make everyone beautiful, but I can make both of these lovebirds look like regular people. They won't be perfect, but they'll still find each other to be pretty slammin', and they'll never want for anyone else. As for their inner beauty, no spell could change that." She turned toward Maddie and the Beast. "Clearly, you've both had that all along. So, do you want to be regular people?"

Maddie and the Beast didn't hesitate. "Yes!" they said in unison.

"Well, fun, fun!" Resplenda said. "Let's get this done!"

Chapter 22

In the garden behind Belle's cottage, everyone in town gathered to celebrate the wedding of two perfectly ordinary, perfectly loving people. The Beast bore a strong resemblance to his old self, but his physique was not perfectly chiseled and muscular like it used to be. He had a bald spot and some lines on his forehead that showed his advancing age.

Maddie allowed herself to have several women dote on her, fixing her hair, and applying makeup, for it was a special occasion and she wanted to look her best. Underneath, though, she was happy with how she looked without all the effort. Every flaw, wrinkle, and blemish was part of who she was and none of them made her the least bit less attractive to the man who loved her more than anything in the world.

The villagers had come to accept both Belle and the Beast for who they were. They no longer judged them for their appearance, but only for the goodness in their hearts. Belle's father marched his daughter proudly down the aisle.

He no longer had any reservations about his daughter marrying the Beast, for he had seen that the love they had for each other was true, and he knew they belonged together.

Beau felt bad when he got his first look at Belle's new appearance. *So much beauty gone to waste*, he thought. But when he saw the look on Belle's face as she gazed into the Beast's eyes, his pity disappeared. He could see the beauty in her heart, and her joy filled Beau with hope that someday, he, too, might find true love.

Jeanette was there as well, but without her notebook. She had spent her career studying the human mind, but even to her, the workings of the heart remained, mostly, a mystery. If Belle was crazy, she concluded, it was only because she was crazy for the Beast.

Sitting at the back of the crowd, Resplenda watched it all, impressed at what the Sweetie Pie and the Snotface had accomplished. She wondered if it was time to lift the curse she had placed on them.

Simone the prison guard felt bad for having mocked Belle, so she showed up to wish her and the Beast well. She wasn't dressed to impress anyone. She just wanted to be comfortable, and she was genuinely happy for the couple.

Perhaps that's why, for the first time, she looked perfectly nice just being herself. She found an open chair and asked the man sitting beside it if she could take it.

"But where will you take it?" he asked her.

He was an odd man for sure, but Simone found him kind of charming and sat down next to him to get to know him better.

Everyone at the wedding agreed that it was a perfect day for an absolutely perfect couple.

Everyone, that is, except the man performing the ceremony.

"Do you, Beast, take you, Beauty, to say sickening lovey-dovey stuff to, have private jokes that aren't funny with, and grow old together until you finally just die already?" The Beast had insisted Holden officiate the wedding, because he was so grateful to him for getting him freed from prison. He didn't realize how much Holden hated the romantic parts of fairy tales.

"And you, Beauty . . ." He looked at Maddie's beaming face. "Oh, come on. We know you'd never do anything to mess this up. Just say 'I do.'"

"I do," Maddie said. She didn't care how rude Holden was being. It was such a perfect day, and the Beast gazed into her eyes so lovingly. She felt much like she did when she first arrived in the fairy tale. She was getting a sneak preview of the happiest day of her life: her wedding day. Her heart began to swell as she realized that any minute now, the Beast would plant a loving kiss on her in front of everyone there. Her first kiss — a wedding kiss! How did she get so lucky?

"Okay, you guys want to see these two get married?" The crowd cheered, and Holden realized he was getting to do something else that always looked kind of fun. "Boom! You're married!" he said. "I guess you can kiss. Just give me a sec to go hit the buffet so I don't have to watch the smoochfest. Ucch!" Holden bolted for the food.

Watching from nearby, Resplenda shook her head, disappointed. He was still a snotface, it seemed, and he still deserved to be cursed. Nonetheless, they had done a good job on this story and it was time to send them back home.

Maddie turned her attention back to the Beast. As the adoring crowd watched, he swept her up in his arms and gazed deeply into her eyes.

"Oh, how I've waited for this moment, Belle. Our first kiss as husband and wife." He leaned down, and Maddie closed her eyes, bursting with anticipation for the most romantic moment of her life. She waited . . . and waited . . . and . . .

"Whew, I'm glad that's over!" Holden said.

Maddie opened her eyes and looked around, only to discover that she and her stepbrother were back in reality, standing in Holden's bedroom.

Chapter 23

Maddie looked at the tablet. If she couldn't live that final romantic moment, she at least wanted to see the illustration. There, on the screen, she saw Belle and the Beast locked in a sweet, magical kiss that looked like it might go on forever. It was so wonderful, so perfect, and it was almost hers. Underneath it were the words she and Holden had been waiting to see:

Happily Ever After.

As sad as Maddie felt to miss out on the kiss, she knew it wasn't hers to have. It was Belle's. It was part of her story, and it was a special moment for her and the Beast. Maddie knew she would have her own first kiss someday. She only hoped it would be as meaningful as Belle's and the Beast's.

"Gross, huh?" Holden said, snatching the tablet away from her. "Why does every fairy tale have to end with a bunch of face sucking?"

"Holden!" Maddie said. "Really? After all we went through, you can't appreciate their kiss?"

"All I see are two people swapping germs and me puking as a result." Holden plugged his tablet into the wall to charge it.

Maddie rolled her eyes. "I think it's a great ending. Now we know they didn't need to be beautiful on the outside to be in love. All they needed was to get to know who they really were inside."

"You know what would've been better?" Holden said. "If they'd both ended up as beasts, and they used their claws to tear apart everyone at the wedding who didn't believe in them. Slash! Slash! Aaah! No! Stop it! Spare our lives!" Holden laughed so hard at his own joke, Maddie could hear Carol stirring from the next room.

"Holden? Are you still awake?"

"No, Mom! I'm, uh, laughing in my sleep!" he said. He climbed into bed, and then whispered to Maddie, "Stop trying to get me in trouble!"

"Okay, go to bed," Maddie said. Surprisingly, she wasn't as annoyed at her stepbrother as she usually was. Much like Belle and the Beast, she had seen another side of him, a deeper Holden beneath the surface.

There might be hope for them to get along as stepsiblings after all.

As she left his room, she bent over him in bed and planted a soft kiss on his cheek.

"Good night, brother," she said.

She walked out to the hallway, and as she opened the door to her own room, she could hear Holden muttering from underneath his blankets, "Don't ever do that again."

He might not exactly be beautiful underneath, but maybe there was something under there worth searching deeper for.

Maybe.

THE END

Turn the page to read
an extract from:

My Rotten
Stepbrother
Ruined Aladdin

There was no sign of Holden for the rest of Maddie's party. He wasn't there for belly dancing or Pin the Hump on the Camel, and he wanted nothing to do with the movie they watched, about the two sick teenagers who fell in love. (Maddie and her teary friends went through three full boxes of tissues during that one.) When he failed to come down for cake, Maddie knew he must be in serious mope mode.

Carol had made each of the birthday kids their own cake, just the way they asked for it. Holden's had black frosting and a scary clown face on it. Instead of *Happy birthday*, the icing spelled out *Holden rulz*. But he refused to come down to blow out the candles.

"I guess we'll just save this until he's feeling up for it," Carol said, putting Holden's cake in the fridge.

"Looks like your birthday wish already came true, Maddie!" Tasha joked as Maddie leaned in to blow out her candles. "Your stepbrother disappeared!"

All the girls laughed, but Maddie felt a pit in her stomach.

As much as Holden drove her nuts, it pained her to think he was spending his birthday sulking in his bedroom, alone. She knew exactly how it felt to want something and to be told she couldn't have it. When she was little, she begged her dad for a fancy doll that he said was just too expensive. Then, there was the home makeover kit that her dad wouldn't buy her because he didn't think she was old enough for makeup.

Maddie took a deep breath and settled on the perfect wish. I wish Holden could get everything he wants for his birthday, she thought to herself, and with one big exhale, she wiped out all twelve candles on her cake.

By 11:00, Maddie's dad had changed out of his genie costume and into his pajamas. "Now I get to grant my own wish," he cracked, "for some peace and quiet!"

As he and Carol went upstairs, Maddie whispered an apology to her friends. "Ugh, my dad's jokes are the worst!"

Now on their own, the girls celebrated their freedom by making microwave popcorn, dimming the living room lights, and telling ghost stories.

Everyone leaned in to hear the gruesome tale, except Maddie, who was distracted by a faint light coming from upstairs, in Holden's bedroom. He was still awake, probably still miserable. As she watched her friends huddle together in fear, she knew just what would cheer up her stepbrother – the chance to sneak in and scare them. All he'd have to do is hide until a tense moment in one of the stories and then jump out and scream, "Boo!" It would actually be kind of funny, so she quietly slipped away to give him the idea.

She made her way upstairs to his bedroom, but before she even had a chance to knock on the door, he croaked, "Go away!"

"But I have an idea," Maddie said. "You could really freak all the girls out."

"Not interested," Holden said. "Good night!"

Maddie sighed. "I'm sorry about the hoverboard. I still think they should've just bought you one."

"I should've asked my dad," Holden replied. "He would've got me one."

Maddie's heart sank. She had forgotten about Holden's father. Not hearing from him all day certainly wasn't helping Holden's mood.

"Come on, we're telling ghost stories," Maddie said. "I'll bet you know some good ones."

Holden responded by turning on loud rock music. He obviously didn't want her sympathy, and he didn't want to be cheered up. He just wanted to be alone.

Even though she knew he couldn't hear her, Maddie whispered, "Happy birthday" through the door. Then she turned around and went back to her party.

Holden couldn't quite make out anything the singer was saying. He wasn't really singing, actually. He was making this deep, guttural scream that shook the walls. Holden thought he heard the word *annihilate*. Maybe there was a *devastation* in the lyrics, too. It may not have made much sense, but it was the perfect music to be angry to. Holden jumped on his bed and nodded his head to the beat. If his mom wouldn't let him go to a Hashtag Number Sign concert, he could at least pretend he was at one. This band kicked butt.

Pretty soon, there was a pounding on the wall. "Holden, headphones, please!" his mom shouted. It was a tired, weak shout. His mom would be an awful rock singer.

Holden strapped on his headphones. Being angry wasn't as fun with headphones on, but that was his only choice right now. It really was the worst birthday ever.

All he wanted was to go to bed, but he couldn't just yet.

He watched the clock, waiting for it to turn midnight. As miserable as it was, he was going to have to spend the entire rest of this horrible day awake.

At midnight, it would be a new day here in Middle Grove, New Jersey. Even better, it would be 6 a.m. in Germany, and that meant his dad would be waking up. It would be the perfect time to video chat with him on his tablet.

His dad would understand how he was feeling. He'd think it was totally lame that his mom didn't get him a hoverboard. He'd probably have one express shipped overseas that day. His dad was cool.

11:59. Holden imagined his dad, probably snoring loudly in a tiny German cottage as the sun came up over the Alps. Was he wearing lederhosen? Probably. That's what people wore to bed in Germany. Any second now, his alarm would go off, and he would wake up, ready to talk to his son.

Holden picked up the tablet to shut off the music. That's when he noticed that the screen was no longer showing the cover of Hashtag Number Sign's album.

It was showing an illustration from *Aladdin*. It was the one thing that could've made this birthday worse.

This was what happened after he criticized a fairy tale.

First, the eBook appeared on his tablet screen. Then, he noticed how the story had changed, and finally, he and Maddie got sucked into the book to fix things.

Not this time.

He turned the tablet over, slid it across his desk, then dumped all his dirty laundry on top of it. He wanted nothing to do with another dumb fairy tale, especially not on the worst birthday of his life.

Maybe he'd get a new tablet. A different brand, a new Wi-Fi network. He'd delete the eBook app. There had to be a way around this curse.

That's when he noticed the clock switching from 11:59 to 12:00. It was the time he'd been waiting for all day. Right now, in Germany, his dad was waking up.

If he wanted to talk to him, he was going to have to look at his tablet again. Sighing deeply, he dug the device out from under his dirty socks and glanced at the screen.

It was still showing *Aladdin*, of course. Holden figured he might as well see what damage he'd done to the story, so he began swiping his way through the pages. It didn't seem that different at first. There was a picture of Aladdin discovering the lamp, just like always. Then came a picture of the genie rolling his eyes, which seemed a little out of character, but nothing major. He turned the next page, and what he saw shocked him so much, he dropped the tablet.

It was a drawing of Aladdin riding a hoverboard.

That's my wish, Holden thought. *If we go into the story,* I'll be Aladdin!

Holden stared at the picture for a long time. Aladdin was hoverboarding — and at the same time chugging an energy drink and eating a pineapple/anchovy/no cheese pizza. No doubt about it. That was him — and he was having the time of his life.

A devious grin broke out on Holden's face. He tucked the tablet under his arm and headed out into the hallway.

All the girls were sleeping downstairs. They looked so silly with drool dripping out of their mouths. He wanted to record the whole thing and put it online for his friends to see. Maddie's friends would be so embarrassed. But there was something more important he had to do first.

He found Maddie and placed the tablet beside her on her sleeping bag. Then, very gently, he slid her left hand over and rested it on the screen.

"Once upon a time," he said, and in an instant, his body began to tingle and shrink.

Maddie's eyes sprung open as she realized what was going on. "Holden?" she said. She watched him get sucked into the tablet's glowing screen. "Why would you—?"

With a whoosh, Maddie was swept up as well. She hovered briefly over her friends before getting sucked into the tablet screen. A couple of the girls stirred at the sound and the flash of light, but all of them settled down and fell back into a deep sleep, unaware that Holden, Maddie, and the tablet had all disappeared from the living room.

About the Author

Jerry Mahoney loves books — reading them, writing them,
and especially ruining them. He has written for and ruined
television shows, newspapers, magazines, and the Internet.
He is excited to finally be ruining something as beloved
as a fairy tale. He lives in Los Angeles with his husband,
Drew, and their very silly children.

About the Illustrator

Aleksei Bitskoff is an Estonian-born British illustrator.
He earned a master's degree in illustration from Camberwell
College of Arts in London. In 2012 he was a finalist for the
Children's Choice Book Award. Aleksei lives in London
with his wife and their young son.

Glossary

anticipate (an-TIS-uh-pate)—expect something to happen

barbarian (bahr-BAIR-ee-uhn)—a rude or violent person

chateau (sha-TOH)—a castle or large country house in France

convey (kuhn-VAY)—tell or communicate

defendant (di-FEN-duhnt)—the person in a court case who has been accused

devastation (dev-uh-STAY-shuhn)—extreme upset

exquisite (ek-SKWIZ-it)—very beautiful with fine features

guillotine (GIL-uh-teen or GEE-uh-teen)—a large machine with a heavy blade, used to cut off the heads of criminals

legitimate (luh-JIT-uh-mit)—reasonable or justified

objection (uhb-JEK-shuhn)—an expression or a feeling of not liking or not approving of something

obnoxious (uhb-NAHK-shuhs)—very unpleasant or annoying in a way that offends people

strategy (STRAT-i-jee)—a clever plan for achieving a goal or winning a game

warrant (WOR-uhnt)—deserve

Think Again

1. Maddie doesn't enjoy her date with Beau, because he doesn't try to get to know her better. Think of three questions Beau could have asked Belle to show that he was interested in who she was. Write a new scene where Beau and Belle have a wonderful date.

2. Holden and Maddie learn that a magical fairy named Resplenda places curses on people to teach them to behave better. Think of someone, real or fictional, who you think needs to learn a lesson in how to behave. What kind of spell do you think Resplenda would cast on him or her, and how would it make the person act differently?

3. The character of Simone goes through some major changes in this story, and that's without being cursed by a magical fairy. Maddie guesses that Simone has fallen in love with the Beast. What clues do you think made Maddie believe this?

Want to Write Great Characters? Try Ruining Yourself!

Here's a secret to creating great characters for your own writing: Don't look so hard! Sometimes, the best characters you can write are closer than you know. You may even find one by looking in the mirror. There's nobody you know better than yourself, after all, and I guarantee you're a pretty interesting person. That means you'd make a great character, too!

Would you believe that I based both Maddie and Holden on myself? It's true. There's a part of me that loves fairy tales. That's why I wanted to write a series about fairy tales in the first place. So when I'm writing Maddie, I think about how that part of my personality would act, how much fun I'd have mixing it up at a royal ball or roaming around Belle's village.

There's another part of me that's more like Holden. That's the part that sees the plot holes in the stories and wonders how to patch them up. Of course, I made Holden far meaner than I am. If he were nice and got along with

Maddie, the story would be dull. So I took a part of my personality and pushed it to an extreme to make it more interesting. I ruined myself!

And you can do the same thing!

Think of everything you'd like about being in a fairy tale. Maybe you'd love living in a castle or not having to go to school. Come up with a character who would enjoy all those same things.

Then think of everything you'd hate about being in the fairy tale. Maybe they have too many dragons or not enough frozen yogurt shops. Now make that a character, too.

Once you know how to make characters out of interesting parts of your own personality, you can do it for any kind of story.

Try ruining your favorite book next. And if it helps, ruin yourself first!

Jerry

FIND MORE MAGICAL STORIES AT WWW.MYCAPSTONE.COM

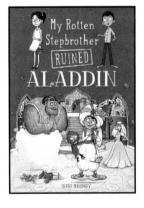

My Rotten Stepbrother RUINED ALADDIN

JERRY MAHONEY

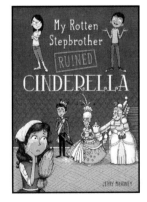

My Rotten Stepbrother RUINED CINDERELLA

JERRY MAHONEY

My Rotten Stepbrother RUINED SNOW WHITE

JERRY MAHONEY